Why
Me

ALSO BY DONALD E. WESTLAKE

Why Me

Donald E. Westlake

THE VIKING PRESS
NEW YORK

LIBRARY OF CONGRESS CATALOGING IN PUBLICATION DATA
Westlake, Donald E.
Why me.
I. Title.
PS3573.E9W5   1983   813'.54   82-10921
ISBN 0-670-76569-4

Printed in the United States of America
Set in Baskerville

DEDICATION

I would like to dedicate this book as follows:

Chapter One is dedicated to Brian Garfield.
Chapter Five is dedicated to Abby Adams.
Chapter Seven is dedicated to Justin Scott.
Chapter Thirty-four is dedicated to Joan Rivers.
Chapter Thirty-five is dedicated to George Movshon.
Chapter Thirty-nine is dedicated to Pete Martin.
Chapter Forty-three is dedicated to Rich Barber.

And all the other Chapters are dedicated to You, dear reader, with my thanks.

They laugh that win.

—John Bartlett, *Familiar Quotations*
(attributed to W. Shakespeare)

Why Me

1

"Hello," said the telephone cheerfully into Dortmunder's ear, "this is Andy Kelp."

"This is Dort—" Dortmunder started to say, but the telephone was still talking in his ear. It was saying:

"I'm not home right now, but—"

"Andy? Hello?"

"—you can leave a message on this recording machine—"

"It's John, Andy. John Dortmunder."

"—and I'll call you back just as soon as I can."

"Andy! Hey! Can you hear me?"

"Leave your message right after you hear the beep. And do have a nice day."

Dortmunder held both hands cupped around the mouthpiece of the phone and roared down its throat: "HELLO!"

"eeeepp"

Dortmunder recoiled from the phone as though it were just about to explode, which he half expected it would. Holding the receiver at arm's length, he watched it mistrustfully for a few seconds, then slowly brought it closer and bent his ear to the earpiece. Silence. A long, hollow, sort of *unreeling* kind of silence. Dortmunder listened, and then there was a faint *click*, and then the silence changed, becoming furry, empty, and pointless. Knowing he was all alone, Dortmunder nevertheless asked, "Hello?" The furry silence went on. Dortmunder hung up the phone, went out to the kitchen, had a glass of milk, and thought it over.

May was out to the movies, so there was no one to discuss this situation with, but on reflection it seemed to Dortmunder pretty clear what had happened. Andy Kelp had got himself a machine to answer the telephone. The question was, why would he do such a thing? Dortmunder cut a slice of Sara Lee cheese danish, chewed it, mulled this question, drank his milk, and at last decided you just could never figure out why Kelp did the things he did. Dortmunder had never talked to a machine before—except for an occasional rude remark at a car that refused to start on a cold morning—but okay; if he was going to continue to know Andy Kelp, he would apparently have to learn to talk to machines. And he might just as well start now.

Leaving the glass in the sink, Dortmunder went back to the living room and dialed Kelp's number again, and this time he didn't start talking until the machine was finished saying, "Hello, this is Andy Kelp. I'm not home right now, but you can leave a message on this recording machine and I'll call you back just as soon as I can. Leave your message right after you hear the beep. And do have a nice day." *eeeepp*

"Sorry you aren't there," Dortmunder said. "This is Dortmunder and I'm—"

But now the machine started talking again: "Hey!" it said. "Hello!"

Probably a malfunction in the announcement mechanism. Well, it wasn't Dortmunder's problem; *he* didn't have any goddam gizmo on his telephone. Doggedly ignoring the machine's irruptions, Dortmunder went on with his message: "—off on a little job. I thought you might come with me—"

"Hey, it's me! It's Andy!"

"—but I guess I can do it on my own. Talk to you later."

As Dortmunder hung up, the phone was saying, rather plaintively, "John? *Hello!*" Dortmunder went to the hall closet, put on his jacket with the burglar tools all tucked away in the hidden interior pockets, and left the apartment. Ten seconds later, in the empty living room, the phone rang. And rang. And rang . . .

2

Nestled on a deep soft background of black velvet, gleaming under the bright glare of the overhead fluorescent tubes, the Byzantine Fire shone a lustrous carmine, reflecting and refracting the light. If machines could bleed, a blood drop from Univac might look like this; cold, clear, almost painfully red, a tiny faceted geodesic dome of deep color and furious light. Weighing ninety carats, the Byzantine Fire was one of the largest and most valuable rubies in the world, worth possibly a quarter million dollars merely in itself, not even counting its setting and its history, both of which were impressive.

The setting for the Byzantine Fire was a large and intricately carved ring of pure gold, in which the central figure of the ruby was surrounded by fourteen tiny blue-and-white sapphires. While this perhaps doubled the overall value, it was the stone's history—ranging through religious wars, thefts, treaties, murders, diplomacy at the highest level, matters of national pride and ethnic identity and theologic significance—that raised it beyond all questions of value; the Byzantine Fire was priceless, like the Kohinoor Diamond.

Therefore, security during this first move of the Byzantine Fire in nearly ninety years was extremely tight. This morning, three separate teams of armed couriers had left the Chicago Natural History Museum, traveling by three different routes to New York City, and not until departure had even the couriers themselves known which team would carry the ring. It was now nearly midnight in New York, and the team with the ring had just been met at the TWA terminal in Kennedy Airport by a security escort from the United States Mission to the United Nations. This new group would carry the ring the rest of the way into Manhattan, to U.S. Mission headquarters in United Nations Plaza, in preparation for tomorrow's ceremony, when the Byzantine Fire would be gravely and solemnly returned to the sovereign nation of Turkey (which in fact had never owned it). After which, thank God, the damn thing would be Turkey's problem.

Until then, however, it remained America's problem, and there was a certain tension among the eight Americans crowded into this small, bare room in the security area of the TWA terminal. In addition to the courier from Chicago with the attaché case chained to his wrist, plus his two bodyguards, there were a three-man escort team from the U.S. Mission and two blasé New York City policemen in uniform, the cops being there simply to represent the city and to observe the ritual of transfer. Nobody *really* expected any trouble.

The Chicago bodyguards began the transfer by turning over their attaché case keys to the New York team, who duly signed receipts. Next, the Chicago courier placed the attaché case on a table and used his own key to remove the handcuff from his wrist. Then he unlocked and opened the attaché case, reached into it, and opened the smaller carrying box within, which was when everybody clustered a bit closer around the table, looking down at the Byzantine Fire, the deep red ruby, the warm encircling gold, the winking little blue-and-white chips of sapphire, all against the black velvet lining of the box. Even the two jaded city cops moved in closer, looking at the ring over the shoulders of the other men. "That's some cherry," one of the cops said.

The balder man from the U.S. Mission frowned at such nonseriousness. "You men should—" he said, and the door behind them opened and four men strode in, wearing black coats and gas masks, lobbing smoke and teargas bombs, carrying Sten guns, and speaking Greek.

3

The jewelry store door said *snnnarrrkkk*. Dortmunder pressed his shoulder against the door, but the *snnnarrrkkk* hadn't done the job. Glancing over his other shoulder—Rockaway Boulevard here in South Ozone Park in the borough of Queens remained empty, the extra wire bypassing the alarm box over the front entrance remained unobtrusive, and the hour remained a quiet midweek midnight—Dortmunder returned his attention to the door, which remained shut.

It was having to be his own lookout that was causing this delay, interrupting his concentration on this blessed door. He'd hoped to have Kelp along for that purpose; too bad he hadn't been home. Since most of the people Dortmunder knew were under the impression that Dortmunder was a jinx—bad luck, rather than incompetence, clouded his days and chilled his nights—it was very tough to find anybody willing to go out with him on a little piece of work. And he didn't want to risk delaying this job another night; who knew how long the owner would be away?

It was the sign in the window—"Closed For Vacation To Serve You Better"—that had first attracted Dortmunder's attention to Skoukakis Credit Jewelers, and when he'd recognized the burglar alarm box over the front door as an old friend, a make and model whose charms he had often rifled over the years, he had felt that destiny was surely—as far too infrequently—smiling on him. Yesterday he'd seen the sign and noted the alarm box, last night he'd studied the lay of the land, and tonight here he was, simultaneously looking over his shoulder and jimmying this infuriating door. "Come *on*," Dortmunder muttered.

snik, responded the door, yawning open so unexpectedly that Dortmunder had to grab the frame to keep from hurtling forward into the Timex watch display.

Sirens. Police sirens. Far distant police sirens, south and east toward Kennedy Airport. Dortmunder paused in the entrance, satisfying himself that the sirens weren't coming his way, and when he saw the headlights of a car that *was* coming this way he stepped into the store, shut the door, and prepared to go to work.

The car stopped, out front. Dortmunder froze, looking through the mesh-covered window in the door, watching the car, waiting for something to happen.

Nothing happened.

Well? A car parks and nothing happens? A moving car comes to a stop at the curb, and then nothing happens? No one climbs out of the car? No one locks the car and walks away to his destination, permitting an honest burglar to get on with his evening's task?

The car's headlights switched off.

There, that was something. And now for something else.

Nothing else. Dortmunder couldn't see how many people were in that car out there, but none of them was in any kind of motion. And until they were, until something else took place, Dortmunder just didn't see how he could with an easy mind proceed with his original program. Not with an occupied car out front. His expression grim with impatience, Dortmunder leaned against the door and looked through the metal mesh—which would shield him from the car's occupants—and waited for those idiots to go away.

Instead of which, they were joined by more idiots. A second car arrived, driving much more hurriedly than the first, angling sharply to park near the curb just ahead of the first car. Two men at *once* hopped out of this car, not even pausing to switch off the headlights. There, that's the way to do it.

And now at last someone also climbed from the first car: one man, from the driver's seat. Like his two more hurried companions, he was dressed in a black coat that was maybe a trifle too heavy for this raw-but-not-cold March night. Unlike them, he seemed in no hurry at all. It was obvious to Dortmunder that this man, as he walked at no great speed around the front of his car to the sidewalk, playing with a ring full of keys, was being exhorted by the other two men to more haste. The slow one nodded, gave soothing patting motions to the air, selected a key, and moved directly toward the jewelry store door.

Holy shit! The jeweler! A stocky older man with a black moustache and black-framed eyeglasses and a black coat, he was coming this way with a key stuck out. Who would end his vacation at such an hour? Twelve-forty a.m., according to all these Timexes. Twelve-forty a.m. on a Thursday. Was *this* a time to reopen for business?

The key rasped in the lock, as Dortmunder faded with careful rapidity deeper into the dark interior of the store. He already knew there was no back exit. Was there a rational hiding place? Was there even a rational explanation for this owner's presence?

(Not for a second did Dortmunder consider that this might be a second set of burglars, perhaps attracted by the same sign. Burglars don't park out front and then just sit there a while. Burglars don't leave their headlights on. And burglars don't just happen to have the right key.)

Fortunately, Dortmunder's jimmying methods did not ruin a door for future use. Had it been bright daylight—had the owner, let us say, returned to his store at a sensible hour tomorrow morning—certain scratches and dents might have been noticeable as he unlocked that door, but in the darkness of twelve-forty a.m. there was nothing to suggest to Mr. Skoukakis, if indeed it was he, that his defenses had been breached. Therefore, as Dortmunder ducked behind a display counter featuring cufflinks employing Roman themes, the calm unlocking continued, the front door opened, and the three men stepped inside, all of them talking at once.

At first Dortmunder assumed the reason he couldn't understand what they were saying was because of their simultaneous transmissions, but then they sorted that out for themselves and began to speak one at a time, and Dortmunder *still* couldn't understand what they were talking about. So it must be some foreign language, though Dortmunder had no idea what. It was all Greek to him.

The two most recent arrivals were doing most of the talking, in quick excited staccato bursts, while the other man—a bit older, slower, more patient—made soothing calm responses. All of this in the dark, since no one had bothered to turn on any lights, for which Dortmunder was thankful. On the other hand, what were these people doing here, talking their foreign language in the dark of a closed jewelry store well after midnight?

Then Dortmunder heard the *plok-chunk* of a safe door being opened, and a very annoyed expression crossed his face. *Were* these burglars? He wished he could rise up above the counter level to see what they were doing over there, but he couldn't chance it. They were between him and the vague illumination from the street, so at best they'd be lumpy silhouettes while he might be identifiably a gray face in motion. So he stayed where he was, and listened, and waited.

Chock-whirrrrr. That was surely the safe door being shut again, and the dial spun. Does a burglar reshut a safe when he's finished with it? Does a burglar spin the dial, to reassure himself that the safe is locked? Shaking his head, hunkering down as comfortably as possible behind the counter, Dortmunder continued to listen, and to wait.

Another flurry of foreign language followed, and then the sound of the door opening, and the voices receded. Dortmunder lifted his head slightly. The voices abruptly dropped to the faintest murmur as the door was slammed shut. A key rattled in the lock.

Dortmunder eased upward, stretching his neck, so that first to appear above the glass counter was his dry, thin hair-colored hair, like dead beach grass in January; then came his narrow forehead, creased with a million old worries; then his pale and pessimistic eyes, looking left and right and straight ahead, like some grim gag-item from a novelty shop.

They were going away. The three men were visible out there, crossing the sidewalk to their respective cars, the older man still slow and methodical, the others still brisk. Those two got into their car first, started the engine with a roar, and had raced away before the older man even got behind the wheel.

Dortmunder moved upward another inch and a half, revealing gaunt cheekbones and a narrow, long crooked nose, the bottom of which he rested on the cool glass of the countertop.

The older man got into his car. A period of time went by. "Maybe," Dortmunder muttered against the wooden sliding door on the back of the display case, "his doctor told him to slow down."

A match flared in the car. It dipped down, then flared up; dipped down, flared up; dipped down, flared up; dipped down. Went out.

A second match flared.

"A pipe smoker," Dortmunder grumbled. "I might of known. We'll be here till sun-up."

Flare-dip; flare-dip; flare-dip. Flare, out.

Pause.

The car engine started, without a roar. After another little interval, the headlights went on. Time passed, and abruptly the car whipped backward two or three feet, then jolted to a stop.

"He put it in the wrong gear," Dortmunder commented. He was beginning to hate that old fart.

The car moved forward. In no hurry at all, it angled away from the curb, joined the stream of no traffic, and disappeared from view.

Bones cracking, Dortmunder unlimbered himself and shook his head. Even a straightforward jewelry store burglary couldn't be simple: mysterious intruders, foreign languages, pipe smokers.

Oh, well, it was over now. Moving forward through the store, Dortmunder brought out his pencil flash, shone it around in brief spurts of light, and found under the cash register the small safe those people had opened and closed. And now Dortmunder smiled, because at least this part of the job was working out. It had seemed to him that any merchant who had bought *that* burglar alarm might very well have bought *this* safe—or one generally like it—and here it was. Another old friend, like the alarm system. Seating himself cross-legged tailor-fashion on the floor in front of this old friend, spreading his tools out around himself, Dortmunder went to work.

It took fifteen minutes, about par for this kind of can. Then the safe door swung open, and Dortmunder beamed his flash in on the trays and compartments. Some nice diamond bracelets, a few okay sets of earrings, an assortment of jeweled brooches, and a varied array of rings. A tray of engagement rings, with diamonds small enough to fall through a cotton sheet; Dortmunder left those behind, but much of the rest went into his various pockets.

And here in this drawer was a little box, which when

open proved to be black velvet lined, and to contain only one item; a ring set with a suspiciously large red stone. Now why would any jeweler put a fake stone like this in his safe? On the other hand, could it possibly be real and yet have found its way to this small-time neighborhood shop?

Dortmunder considered leaving the thing, but then decided he might just as well take it along. The fence would tell him if it was at all valuable.

Stowing the swag and his tools into the various pockets of his jacket, Dortmunder got to his feet and spent a minute longer in the place, shopping. What would be nice for May? Here was a ladies' digital watch, with a simulated platinum band; you pressed this button here on the side, and on the TV-screen-shaped black face numbers appeared, telling you the exact time down to hundredths of a second. Very useful for May, who happened to be a supermarket cashier. And what made it a *ladies'* watch, the numbers were pink.

Dortmunder pocketed the watch, took one last look around, saw nothing else of interest, and left. He did not bother to close the safe.

Georgios Skoukakis hummed a little tune as he drove his maroon Buick Riviera northeastward across Queens toward Belmont Race Track and Floral Park and his own tidy little home near Lake Success. He had to smile when he thought how excited those two men had been, so nervous and keyed up. Here were they, experienced guerrillas, soldiers, fighters in Cyprus, young men barely in their thirties, healthy, professional and well-armed. And on the other hand here was himself, Georgios Skoukakis, 52, naturalized American citizen, jeweler, small merchant, no history of violence or guerrilla activity, never even in the Army, and who was it stayed calm?

Who was it had to say, "Easy, easy, gentlemen, haste makes waste"? Who was it behaved naturally, normally, calmly, holding the Byzantine Fire in the palm of his hand as though it were an everyday event, placing it in the safe in his shop as though it were nothing more than a fairly expensive watch brought in for repair? Who was it but Georgios Skoukakis himself, smiling a comfortable smile as he drove through quiet Queens streets, puffing his second-favorite pipe, humming a little self-congratulatory tune.

Unlike most countries, which are merely two nations—North and South Korea, East and West Germany, Christian and Moslem Lebanon, white and black South Africa, Israel and Palestine, the two Cypruses, the two Irelands—the United States is several hundred nations, all coexisting like parallel universes or multilayered plywood on the same messily drawn rectangle which is America. There's the Boston Ireland, the Miami Beach Israel, the northern California Italy, the southern Florida Cuba, the Minnesota Sweden, the Yorkville Germany, the Chinas in every large city, the East Los Angeles Mexico, the Brooklyn Puerto Rico, a whole lot of Africas, and the Pittsburgh Poland, to name a few.

The natives of these countries carry their dual allegiances very lightly for the most part, hardly ever worrying about potential conflict, and always equally prepared to serve whichever of their nations has need of them. Thus the IRA in the original Ireland is financed and armed by the Irish in the American Ireland. Thus the furtherance of Puerto Rican independence is abetted by the blowing up of New York bars. And thus, a Greek-born naturalized American jeweler is available for assistance in the Greco-Turkish squabble over Cyprus.

Georgios Skoukakis, in addition to the usual watch mending and engagement-ring peddling of the jeweler's trade, had a sideline which had now become useful to his other nation. From time to time he still visited the old country, and he always combined business with pleasure by transporting jewelry in both directions—all perfectly legal, since prior to the first such trip several years ago he had applied for and obtained all the necessary permissions and licenses. Over the years he had helped to finance many a pleasant vacation by transporting digital watches to Salonika and returning with old gold.

Tomorrow, another such trip would take place. The bags were packed, the reservations made, everything was ready. He and Irene would arise in the morning, drive to Kennedy Airport (with a pause at the shop, just a few blocks out of the way), then leave the car in the long-term parking lot, take the free bus to the terminals, and smoothly board the Olympic Airways morning flight for Athens. And on this trip, in among the charm bracelets and earrings yawned over by the bored Customs inspectors, would be a mixed assortment of somewhat garish costume jewelry, featuring large fake stones.

The boldness of this plan was its strongest asset. The least likely route for the Byzantine Fire, of course, would be a round trip directly back to the same airport from which it had been stolen. Even so, very few individuals would be able to clear a large red-stoned ring through the Customs officials of *any* airport in America tomorrow morning; Georgios Skoukakis was perhaps uniquely qualified for the task. How fortunate that he also happened to be such a calm and reliable and steady man.

Turning onto Marcum Lane, Georgios Skoukakis was a bit surprised to notice light in the living room windows of his house, but then he smiled to himself, realizing that Irene too was probably feeling tense tonight, unable to sleep, and was waiting up for his return. Which was fine; it would be pleasant to talk with her, tell her about the excitable young men.

He didn't bother to put the car in the garage, leaving it in the driveway for the morning. Crossing the lawn, he paused to light his pipe—puff, puff, puff. His hands were absolutely steady.

Irene must have seen him through the window, for as he crossed the porch she opened the front door. Her tense and strained expression told him he'd been right; she was quite upset, much more nervous about this adventure than she'd earlier let on.

"Everything's fine, Irene," he assured her, as he stepped into the house, turned, paused, blinked, and the bottom fell out of his throat. He stared through the archway into the living room at two tall slender men in topcoats and dark suits who were getting to their feet from the flower-pattern armchairs and walking this way. The younger one had a moustache. The older one was holding out his wallet, showing identification, saying, "FBI, Mr. Skoukakis. Agent Zachary."

"I confess," Georgios Skoukakis cried. "I did it!"

May was sitting in the living room, squinting through cigarette smoke and doing the quiz in the latest *Cosmopolitan.* Dortmunder shut the door and she squinted across the room at him, saying, "How'd it go?"

"Okay. Nothing special. How was the movie?"

"Nice. It was about a hardware store in Missouri in 1890. Beautiful shots. Terrific period feeling."

Dortmunder didn't share May's enthusiasm for movies; his question had been merely polite. He said, "The owner came in while I was in the store."

"No! What happened?"

"I guess he was the owner. Him and two other guys. Came in for a minute, fooled around, left. Didn't even turn the lights on."

"That's weird." She watched him empty bracelets and rings out of his pockets onto the coffee table. "Some nice stuff."

"I got you something." He handed her the watch. "You press the button on the side."

She did so: "Nice. Very nice. Thank you, John."

"Sure."

She pressed the button again. "It says ten after six."

"Yeah?"

"How do I set the time?"

"I don't know," Dortmunder said. "I didn't see any instructions. It was the display model."

"I'll figure it out," she said. She twiddled the button, then pressed it again. Clouds of cigarette smoke enveloped her head from the eighth-of-an-inch butt in the corner of her mouth. She put the watch down, took another crumpled cigarette from the pocket of her gray cardigan, and lit it from the ember she removed from her lower lip.

Dortmunder said, "You want anything?"

"No, thanks, I'm set."

Dortmunder went away to the kitchen and came back with a bourbon and water and a small white plastic bag. "Figure out the watch?"

"I'll look at it later." She had been frowning at the quiz again, and now she said, "Would you say I am *very* dependent, *somewhat* dependent, *slightly* dependent, or *not at all* dependent?"

"That depends." On one knee, he scooped the loot from the coffee table into the plastic bag. "I'll take this stuff over to Arnie in the morning."

"Andy Kelp called."

"He's got some kind of machine on his phone."

"He says please call him in the morning."

"I don't know if I want to keep talking to a machine forever." He tied shut the top of the plastic bag, put it on the coffee table, picked up the watch and pressed the button. Pink LED digits said 6:10:42:08. He twiddled the button, pressed it again: 6:10:42:08. "Hm," he said.

May said, "I'll put *slightly* dependent."

Dortmunder yawned. Putting the watch down, he said, "I'll look at it in the morning."

"I mean," May said, "nobody's *not at all* dependent."

6

Malcolm Zachary loved being an FBI man. It gave a certain meaningful tension to everything he did. When he got out of a car and slammed the door, he didn't do it like just anybody, he did it like an FBI man: step, swing, slam, a fluid motion, flex of muscle, solid and determined, graceful in a manly sort of way. Malcolm Zachary got out of cars like an FBI man, drank coffee like an FBI man, sat quietly listening like an FBI man. It was terrific; it gave him a heightened self-awareness of the most delicious sort, like suddenly seeing yourself on closed-circuit television in a store window. It went with him through life, everywhere, in everything he did. He brushed his teeth like an FBI man—shoulders squared, elbow up high and sawing left and right, *chick-chick, chick-chick*. He made love like an FBI man—ankles together, elbows bearing the weight, *hum*-pah, *hum*-pah.

He also, Malcolm Zachary, questioned a suspect like an FBI man, which in the present circumstance was perhaps unfortunate. While Zachary couldn't remember any suspect ever collapsing quite so rapidly as Georgios Skoukakis, it was unfortunately true that he could also not remember any suspect ever clamming up again quite so fast. One statement— "FBI, Mr. Skoukakis. Agent Zachary"—and the suspect had opened up like a landing craft: "I confess! I did it!" But then came the first question—"We'll want the names of your associates"—and the landing craft immediately snapped reshut and rusted into place.

Having an awareness of other people that was less heightened than his awareness of himself, Zachary had no idea what had gone wrong. He didn't know how fragile and false had been that self-deception in Georgios Skoukakis' brain which he, Zachary, had destroyed by his mere presence. On the other hand he had no clue to the roiled tumble of emotions coursing through the poor man immediately after his blurted confession: the humiliation, the self-contempt, re-

gret, horror, despair, the knowledge that he had now destroyed everything forever, with no hope of ever ever *ever*
repairing the damage he had done.

"We'll want the names of your associates."

Bang! Instant redemption. Georgios Skoukakis had destroyed *himself* forever, but valor was still possible. He would
not betray his associates. Zachary could have put bamboo
shards under Skoukakis' fingernails, burning coals between
his toes—he wouldn't, of course, that not being the FBI way,
but just as a hypothetical—and Georgios Skoukakis would not
betray his associates. Very seldom is it given to a man, having
failed, to atone for his failure quite so rapidly as in the case of
Georgios Skoukakis.

Of none of which was Zachary aware. He knew only that
Skoukakis had cracked at the first tap of the shell. So now
Zachary was standing here, ballpoint pen in right hand, notebook in left hand (exactly like an FBI man), waiting for the
answer to his first question and not yet aware that the answer
was not going to come. He prodded a bit: "Well?"

"Never," said Georgios Skoukakis.

Zachary frowned at him. "I beg your pardon?"

"Never."

Zachary's partner, a younger man with a moustache
named Freedly— Well, no. The *man* was named Freedly.

Zachary's partner, a younger man named Freedly with a
moustache—

Zachary's partner, a moustached younger man named
Freedly—

Freedly said, "Have you got the ring on you?"

"Just a minute, Bob," Zachary said. "Let's get the answer to this other question first."

"He won't answer that question, Mac," Freedly said.
"Well, Mr. Skoukakis? Is it on you?"

"No," said Skoukakis.

Zachary said, "What do you mean, he won't answer it?"

The suspect's wife, Irene Skoukakis, said something
short, fast, and probably vicious in a foreign language, no
doubt Greek.

"None of that," Zachary told her.

Skoukakis looked terribly ashamed of himself. "I'm sorry, Irene," he said. "I just wasn't man enough."

This time the wife spoke one word in English.

"None of that either," Zachary told her.

Freedly said, "Where is it, Mr. Skoukakis?"

Skoukakis sighed. "In my shop," he said.

"I would like," Zachary said, "to return to the interrogation. I asked a question."

"He won't answer it," Freedly said. "Let's go get the ring."

Zachary frowned like an FBI man. "What?"

"It's in his shop," Freedly said. "That's the point, isn't it? He won't give us any names, Mac, so let's forget that and go get the ring. Come along, Mr. Skoukakis."

Zachary didn't dislike Freedly—it would not have been possible for him to dislike a fellow FBI man—but there were moments when his liking for Freedly became less than perfect. Freedly didn't always behave like a proper FBI man, which left Zachary at times out in limbo someplace, being an FBI man all on his own while Freedly was just sort of *doing* things. Like now—fifteen or twenty minutes of interrogation bypassed completely, and they were merely going to get the ring. Zachary said, "What about the wife?"

"She isn't going anywhere," Freedly said. "Are you, Mrs. Skoukakis?"

Irene Skoukakis was a bit old to smolder, but she managed. "I shall get a divorce," she said. "But first I shall be unfaithful with a Turk."

Her husband moaned.

"Let's go," Freedly said.

Okay, okay; Zachary turned the pages, skipped ahead, found his place, and said, like an FBI man, "Right. Let's go get that ring. Come along, Skoukakis."

"Good night, Irene."

Zachary and Freedly and the suspect went outside, and the wife slammed the door very hard after them. Their agency car, an avocado Pontiac, was across the street under a maple tree. They started in that direction and Skoukakis said, "Do you want to follow me?"

Zachary didn't understand the question. Apparently Freedly did, though, because he grinned at Skoukakis and said, "Oh, no, Mr. Skoukakis. You'll ride *with* us."

"Oh, yes," Skoukakis said. "Of course. I wasn't thinking."

"Naturally you'll ride with us," Zachary said, having caught up. "What are you trying to pull?"

"Nothing," Skoukakis said.

Freedly drove, Zachary and Skoukakis riding in back, Skoukakis giving directions to his store. Freedly radioed in while they were stopped at a red light, saying, "We picked up Skoukakis. He says the object is at his shop. We're on the way there with him."

"Wrapping it up fast," said the radio, in a loud, distorted, but cheerful voice. "That's the way to do it."

"You bet," Freedly said. He stopped talking on the radio and drove the car forward.

Skoukakis said, "Excuse me."

"You were on our list," Freedly told him.

"Ah," Skoukakis said.

Zachary frowned. "What?"

"I didn't know you had a list," Skoukakis said.

"We've got lots of lists," Freedly told him. "The hit squad was Greek. It seemed political rather than criminal. They'd want to get it out of the country, and you were one of the likelier possibilities."

"The FBI has its methods," Zachary said. He'd caught up again.

At the shop, Skoukakis unlocked the door and went in first, switching on the lights and then stopping dead. "Move along," Zachary said.

Skoukakis cried out in Greek. He ran forward. Zachary made a grab for him but missed, and Skoukakis stopped again.

"Oh, for Christ's sake," Freedly said. "Say it isn't so."

Zachary said, "What?"

Skoukakis turned toward them a dead-white face and gestured at his open safe. "I've been robbed!"

"Shit," said Freedly, and went out to the car to call in.

Zachary said, "What?"

7

Dortmunder's breakfast was: sweetened grapefruit juice (at which he made a face), two fried eggs over *hard*, white bread toasted with apricot preserves, instant coffee with a lot of milk and sugar. He had finished everything but the second piece of toast and the third cup of coffee when May came into the kitchen, wearing her coat. "Don't forget to call Andy Kelp," she said.

Dortmunder was fiddling with the digital watch. "Mm," he said, and pressed the button on the side; the pink numbers said 6:10:42:08. "Mm," he said.

"You'll be home for dinner?"

"Yeah. I'll take that stuff over to Arnie this morning. Maybe we'll eat out."

"That'd be nice," she said, and left the kitchen.

Dortmunder drank some coffee, turned the watch around and around in his hands, poked it a bit, and pressed the button on the side. 6:10:42:08.

The front door closed.

Dortmunder chewed toast and considered the watch. When you weren't pressing the button on the side, the rectangular black face was blank; it looked like Dick Tracy's wrist TV. Dortmunder held the watch near his mouth. "Hello, Tess?" he said. "This is Tracy."

The phone rang.

Dortmunder removed the remaining toast from his mouth by drinking the remaining coffee, patted his lips with a paper napkin, and walked into the living room. He picked up the phone on the fifth ring. "Yeah," he said.

"What took so long?"

"Hello, Andy."

"You were in the kitchen, I bet." The real Andy Kelp sounded just as cheery as the machine Andy Kelp.

"You got a machine on your phone," Dortmunder accused him.

"You want an extension for your kitchen?"

"What do you want with a machine on your phone?"

"It'd save you steps. I could install it myself, you wouldn't pay any monthly fee."

"I don't need an extension," Dortmunder said firmly, "and you don't need a machine."

"It's very useful," Kelp said. "If there's people I don't want to talk to, I don't talk to them."

"I already do that," Dortmunder said, and the phone went *guk-ick, guk-ick, guk-ick*. "Now what?" Dortmunder said.

"Hold on," Kelp told him. "Somebody's calling me."

"Somebody's calling you? You're calling me." But Dortmunder was speaking into a dead phone. "Hello?" he said. "Andy?" Then he shook his head in disgust, hung up, and went back to the kitchen to make another cup of coffee. The water was just boiling when the phone rang. He turned off the flame, walked back to the living room, and answered on the fourth ring. "Yeah," he said.

"Wha'd you hang up for?"

"I didn't hang up. You hung up."

"I told you hold on. That was just my call-waiting signal."

"Don't tell me about these things."

"It's terrific," Kelp said. "Say we're talking like this—"

"Yeah."

"And somebody else wants to call me. Instead of a busy signal, the phone rings. That's the click-click you heard."

"It wasn't click-click, it was *guk-ick*."

"Well, whatever. The point is, I've got this button on the phone here, and I press it to put you on hold and answer this

other call. Then I tell them I'll call them back, or whatever I
do, and I press the button again, and we go on with our
conversation, same as ever."

"We could go on with our conversation same as ever
without all that stuff."

"But I'd miss that other call."

"Andy," Dortmunder said, "if you want to call me, and
the line's busy, what do you do?"

"I hang up."

"*Then* what do you do?"

"I call back."

"So I didn't miss the call, did I?"

"But this is more efficient."

"Fine," said Dortmunder. Another argument saved.

"See what it is," Kelp said, "I got access— You know
what I mean?"

"Access. You can get into."

"Right. It's a wholesaler for telephone equipment. Not
the phone company; you know, one of those private companies."

"Yeah."

"Their warehouse fronts on the street behind me."

"Ah," said Dortmunder.

"I got *lots* of stuff."

"Terrific."

"I got— You know how I just dialed your number?"

"With your nose?"

"Heh, heh. That's pretty good. Listen, lemme tell you. I
got these cards. I got this card with holes punched in it for
your telephone number, and I put the card in a slot in this
phone here, and the *card* dials the number."

"More efficient," Dortmunder said.

"You got it. I got phones now all— You know where I'm
calling you from?"

"The closet?"

"The bathroom."

Dortmunder closed his eyes. "Let's talk about something
else," he said

"You know, I was home here when you called yesterday." Kelp sounded a bit aggrieved.

"Not according to the machine."

"I kept trying to tell you it was me."

"You said you were the machine."

"No, *afterward*. Did you do the thing?"

"Yeah."

"Who with?"

"Single-o."

Kelp chuckled, and said, "You didn't do the big jewel thing out to Kennedy, did you?"

Skoukakis Credit Jewelers was near Kennedy Airport. Dortmunder said, "How'd you know? Was it in the papers?"

"In the— John, are you—" *Guk-ick, guk-ick, guk-ick.* "Oop! Hold on."

"No," said Dortmunder, and hung up, and went back to the kitchen and turned the heat on under the kettle. He rinsed his breakfast dishes, and the water was just boiling when the phone rang. He went ahead and made coffee, added lots of milk and sugar, stirred, put the spoon in the sink, walked back to the living room, and picked up the phone on the fourteenth ring. "Yeah."

"What's the *matter* with you?"

"I was making coffee."

"You need an extension in the kitchen."

"No, I don't. Who was your other call?"

"A wrong number."

"Good thing you didn't miss it."

"Well, anyway. Where were you last night?"

"Where you said. Out by Kennedy."

"Come on, John," Kelp said. "Don't milk the joke."

"Milk what joke?"

Sounding exasperated, Kelp said, "You did not steal some twenty-million-dollar ruby from Kennedy Airport last night."

"That's right," Dortmunder said. "Who said I did?"

"*You* did. I make a joke about the big heist at Kennedy last night, and you—"

"I was out near Kennedy. Right."

"Not *near* Kennedy. *At* Kennedy."

"Oh. It was a misunderstanding."

"So what you hit was a—"

"Andy."

"What?"

"You maybe aren't the only one who puts little extras on their phones."

"There's something you want?"

"You ever hear of wiretap?"

"Who do you want tapped?"

"Nobody. But let's just pretend, just for fun, let's just make believe the police or somebody have tapped your phone or my phone or whatever."

"For what?"

"Oh, to find out if either one of us happened to commit a crime recently."

"Oh. I see what you mean."

"Also," Dortmunder said, "there is no such thing as a twenty-million-dollar ruby."

"Valuable," Kelp said. "Priceless. It's in the papers and on television and everything."

"I wasn't thinking that big last night," Dortmunder said, and the phone went *guk-ick, guk-ick, guk-ick.* "That's it," Dortmunder said. "Good-bye."

"John! Just hold on a second!"

Dortmunder hung up and carried his coffee back to the kitchen and sat at the table and studied the watch some more. 6:10:42:08.

The phone rang.

Dortmunder turned the watch around and around in his hands. He sipped coffee.

The phone went on ringing.

Dortmunder hit the watch against the tabletop, then pressed the button on its side: 6:10:42:09. "Ah-hah," Dortmunder said. He looked at the clock on the kitchen wall—eleven-fifteen, more or less—and waited while the sweep second hand went halfway round the face. (The phone still

rang.) Then he pressed the button on the side of the watch.
6:10:42:09.

"Mm," said Dortmunder. He hit the watch against
the tabletop, pressed the button. 6:10:42:10. Hit; press.
6:10:42:11.

Fine. If you started at ten minutes after six, and if you
hit this watch against the tabletop six thousand times a minute, it'd keep perfect time. Leaving the watch on the table,
Dortmunder went to the living room, walked past the ringing
phone, put on his other jacket—the one with no tools in it—
put the plastic bag with last night's proceeds in his pocket,
and left the apartment.

You don't get to be top cop in the great city of New York by
squattin back on your heels and spittin between your knees;
no, sir. You get to be top cop in the great city of New York by
standin up four-square with your fists at the ready and smash-
in the face of every pest and nuisance as gets in your way,
bedad. And by then you're makin enough money—with your
salary and what dibs of undeclared cash happen to fall from
time to time into your open palm—so you no longer have to
live in that smelly awful city of New York at all any more, but
can have a lovely big house in Bay Shore, out in Suffolk
County on Long Island, a nice water-frontage house lookin
out at Great South Bay. And you can have your own power
boat (called *Lucille*, after your wife, to keep her quiet), and
three ungrateful children, and a summer cottage over on the
beach at Fire Island, and a beer belly, and the satisfaction of
knowin you've done about the best any man could do with
the hand you were dealt.

Nine-thirty a.m. Chief Inspector Francis Xavier Mologna (pronounced Maloney), having driven into the city

three hours earlier than his usual habit, and having been rigorously briefed for the last thirty minutes, followed his beer belly into the big conference room at Headquarters (One Police Plaza, downtown behind City Hall, a lovely building, all tall and dark brick, built like a giant pinup), and got introduced to a lot of damn new faces. There was no way a man could remember all those names, but fortunately Chief Inspector Mologna didn't have to; he was accompanied by Leon, his secretary, whose job it was to remember things like that and who happened to be very good at it.

But what a lot of people had crowded into this conference room for this conference. Most of them men, most of them white, but here and there women, here and there black. In addition to Chief Inspector Mologna and Leon and two detectives from New York's finest, there were also representatives from the Housing Police, the Transit Police, the DA's office, the State CID, the FBI, the CIA, the United States Mission to the United Nations, United States Customs, the Chicago Natural History Museum, Turkish Intelligence, and the Turkish Mission to the United Nations. The first fifteen or twenty minutes of the meeting was just spent with people introducing themselves to one another. "Pronounced Maloney," Mologna kept saying, and relied on Leon to remember who everybody was.

An FBI man named—Mologna raised an eyebrow at Leon, seated to his left at the long oval conference table, who wrote *Zachary* on his yellow pad—Zachary got the ball rolling by standing up and telling them what they all already knew: some son of a bitch had stolen the Byzantine Fire, and some *other* son of a bitch had stolen it from the first son of a bitch. Zachary had a graphic display—charts and blown-up photographs one after another on an easel—and a pointer, and a kind of stiff mechanical way of pointing at things with the pointer, as though he weren't quite a human being but was a model put together by the Walt Disney people. A Walt Disney FBI man. "We know," this fellow (squint at legal pad) Zachary said, "that the first group was Greek Cypriot. Several individuals are already in custody, and the rest should be

rounded up soonest. So far, no hard information is available
on the second group, though several theories have been advanced."

You just bet they have, Mologna thought. He caught
Leon's eye and they shared a millisecond twinkle. It was
amazing how their minds meshed like that. Here was Chief
Inspector Francis Xavier Mologna (pronounced Maloney), 53
years of age, a God-fearing white male Long Island Irishman,
and be *damned* if the person in all of life whose thought pro-
cesses most closely matched his own wasn't some damn 28-
year-old smart-aleck faggot nigger called Sergeant Leon
Windrift. (Had Leon been only homosexual, he would have
been bounced out of New York's finest long ago. Had he been
only black, he'd be a patrolman forever. Being a faggot *and* a
nigger, he could neither be fired nor kept in some damn precinct, which is why he'd risen so rapidly through the ranks to
a sergeantcy and a job at Headquarters, where Mologna had
first noticed him and stolen him for himself.)

"One suggestion," the FBI man—Zachary—was saying,
"has been that a *second* Greek Cypriot group was responsible
for the second purloinment."

Purloinment?

"The advantage of this theory is that it explains how the
second group had so thoroughly infiltrated the first group as
to be aware of their intended disposition of the ruby. There
are contending factions, of course, within the umbrella groupage of Greek Cypriot nationalism."

Groupage?

"A second theory proposed has been that agents of the
Soviet Union, pursuant to the claims earlier put forward by
the Russian Orthodox Church in re annexment of the Byzantine Fire, were responsible for the second theft."

Annexment?

"In support of this theory is the fact that the USSR Mission to the United Nations has already denied Russian complicacy in the events of last evening. However, a third
potentialism would be a transactage by a dissident factor
within the Turkish populace."

Complicacy?

Potentialism?

Transactage?

"Colonel Bubble of Turkish Intelligence—"

Mologna raised an eyebrow at Leon, who wrote on his yellow pad *Bubul.*

"—has assured us of the unlikelihood of this eventuation, but he will keep it under some advisement."

Oh, well.

"Fourthly, there is always the possibility of coincidentalistic activity. A mere burglar may have stumbled upon the Byzantine Fire whilst engaged in his own depredatory activities. If there are any further suggestions anyone here might care to make, additional theories as to the perpetrators, their motivations, their future intentionisms, we'll all be happy to hear them."

Oh, will we? Mologna and Leon did the eye thing again.

"In the meantime," Zachary was saying, pointing this way and that randomly with his pointer, "as both felonies were perpetrated within the parameters of the city of New York, they come within the primary jurisdiction of the New York City police force, which will coordinate interagency activities and assume transcendent responsibility for the investigation. Therefore, I am happy at this time to turn the meeting over to Chief Inspector Mo-log-na of the New York City police."

Grunting, Mologna heaved himself to his feet and rested his beer belly on the table. "It's pronounced Maloney," he said. "You people can have your theories, and you can run down a lot of Greeks and Turks and Russian Orthodoxes, but I'll tell you right now what happened. That damn fool jeweler put a sign in his window that he was leavin town. Perfect invitation to a burglar. There was a nice little piece of wire put on the alarm to bypass it. The door was jimmied open as gentle as a weddin night. The safe was cracked by a professional cracksman. He took this damn ruby ring we're all so excited about, but he didn't know what it was because he *also* took a lot of penny-ante rings and bracelets and watches.

Your terrorists and dissidents and all them types don't know how to quiet a burglar alarm or ease open a safe. All they know is machine guns and Molotov cocktails and a lot of noise and fuss and blood. It's a nice New York hometown burglar is what we're lookin for, and I tell you right now I'll find him. My boys'll toss this entire goddam city, we'll pick up every grifter and drifter and peterman and second-story man in town, we'll shake em all by the heels, and when you hear a *plink*, that'll be the ring fallin out of somebody's pocket. In the meantime, anybody got any questions, you deal with Sergeant Windrift here, my secretary. Now, if you'll excuse me, I've got a whole lot of arrestin to do."

And Chief Inspector Mologna followed his beer belly out of the conference room.

There was a *Daily News* on the seat on the subway, but Dortmunder didn't read about the big jewel robbery out to Kennedy. Other people's successes didn't interest him that much. Instead he leafed through to page seven, where he read about three guys in Staten Island who went into a bar last night to hold it up and the customers jumped all over them and threw their guns into the Kill Van Kull and let the air out of the tires of their getaway car, but then when the cops showed up (called by some busybody neighbor bugged by the noise) none of the customers would say which three guys in their midst were the holdup men, so the cops arrested everybody and it still hadn't been sorted out. The bartender, claiming it was too dim in the bar to see which of his customers was holding him up, was quoted as saying, "Anyway, it was just youthful exuberance."

Dortmunder was on the BMT. At 28th Street four cops came aboard and the doors stayed open until the cops found

the two guys they wanted. Dortmunder sat there behind his
News, reading about a pantyhose sale at Alexander's, and the
cops grabbed these two guys from just across the aisle and
frisked them and marched them out of the train. Just two
ordinary guys, like you see around. Then the doors closed and
the train moved on, and Dortmunder came out from behind
his paper to watch the cops walking the two guys away across
the receding platform.

At Times Square he changed for the Broadway IRT, and
there seemed to be cops sort of strolling around all over the
station—a lot more than the usual sprinkle. The plastic bag of
jewelry in Dortmunder's pocket was getting heavier and
heavier. It was making, he thought, a very obvious bulge. He
walked with his right arm close against his side, but that
might draw attention too, so then he walked with his right
arm elaborately moving, but that could also draw attention,
so finally he just slunk along, not giving a damn if he drew
attention or not.

At 86th Street, when he came up out of the subway,
right there by the bank building on the corner at Broadway
two cops had a guy leaning against the wall and were giving
him a toss. It all was beginning to seem like a bad omen or
something. "Probably everything I grabbed was paste," Dortmunder muttered to himself, and walked up to 89th Street
between Broadway and West End, where Arnie had an apartment up over a bookstore. Dortmunder rang the bell, and
Arnie's voice came out of the metal grid, saying, "Who is it?"

Dortmunder leaned close to the grid: "It's me."

"Who the hell is me?"

Dortmunder looked around the tiny vestibule. He looked
out at the street. He leaned as close to the grid as he could get
and mumbled, "Dortmunder."

Very very loud, the voice of Arnie yelled from the grid,
"*Dortmunder?*"

"Yeah. Yeah. Okay? Yeah."

The door went click-click-click, and Dortmunder pushed
on it and went into the hallway, which always smelled of old
newspapers. "Next time I'll just pick the lock," he muttered,

and went upstairs, where Arnie was waiting in his open doorway.

"So," Arnie said. "You scored?"

"Sure."

"Sure," Arnie said. "Nobody comes to see Arnie just to
say hello."

"Well, I live way downtown," Dortmunder said, and
went on into the apartment, which had small rooms with big
windows looking out past a black metal fire escape at the
brown-brick back of a parking garage maybe four feet away.
Part of Arnie's calendar collection hung around on all the
walls: Januaries that started on Monday, Januaries that
started on Thursday, Januaries that started on Saturday.
Here and there, just to confuse things, were calendars that
started with August or March; "incompletes," Arnie called
them. Above the Januaries (and the Augusts and the
Marches) sunlit icy brooks ran through snowy woods, sug-
gestively smirking girls inefficiently struggled with blowing
skirts, pairs of kittens looked out of wicker baskets full of balls
of wool, and various Washington monuments (the White
House, the Lincoln Memorial, the Washington Monument)
glittered like teeth in the happy sunshine.

Closing the door, following Dortmunder, Arnie said,
"It's my personality. Don't tell me different, Dortmunder, I
happen to know. I rub people the wrong way. Don't argue
with me."

Dortmunder, who'd had no intention of arguing with
him, found Arnie rubbing him the wrong way. "If you say
so," he said.

"I do say so," Arnie said. "Sit down. Sit down at the
table there, we'll look at your stuff."

The table was in front of the parking-garage-view windows. It was an old library table on which Arnie had laid out
several of his less valuable incompletes, fixing them in place
with a thick layer of clear plastic laminate. Dortmunder sat
down and rested his forearms on a September 1938. (A shy-
but-proud boy carried a shy-but-proud girl's schoolbooks
down a country lane.) Feeling vaguely pressed to demonstrate

some sort of comradeliness, Dortmunder said, "You're lookin pretty good, Arnie."

"Then my face lies," Arnie said, sitting across the table. "I feel like shit. I been farting a lot. That's why I keep this window open, otherwise you'd faint when you walked in here."

"Ah," said Dortmunder.

"Not that a whole hell of a lot of people *do* walk in here," Arnie said. "People don't want to know me, I'm such a pain in the ass. Believe me, I know what I'm talking about."

"Uh," said Dortmunder.

"I read things sometimes in the *Sunday News*—Do Your Friends Think You're A Turd? shit like that—I follow the advice three four days, maybe a week, but my own rotten self always comes through in the end. I could see you in a bar today, I could buy you a beer, talk about *your* problems, ask questions about *your* livelihood, express an interest in *your* personality, and tomorrow you'd go to a different bar."

That was undoubtedly true. "Uh," repeated Dortmunder, that being the most noncommittal sound he knew how to make.

"Well, you already know all this," Arnie said. "The only reason you'll put up with me, I give good dollar. And I gotta give good dollar or I'd *never* see anybody. There's people right now in this city go to Stoon even though he gives a worse dollar—they'll take smaller cash just so they don't have to sit and talk with Arnie."

Dortmunder said, "Stoon? Which Stoon is this?"

"Even you," Arnie said. "Now you want Stoon's address."

Dortmunder did. "No, I don't, Arnie," he said. "We got a good relationship." Trying to change the subject, he took the plastic bag out of his pocket and emptied the goods onto the schoolchildren. "This is the stuff," he said.

Reaching for it, Arnie said, "Good relationship? I don't have a good relationship with any—"

There was a sudden loud knocking at the door. In relief, Dortmunder said, "See? There's somebody come to visit."

Arnie frowned. He yelled over at the door, "Who is it?"

A loud, firm voice yelled back, "Police, Arnie! Open up!"

Arnie gave Dortmunder a look. "My friends," he said. Getting to his feet, slowly strolling toward the door, he yelled, "Whada *you* people want?"

"Open it up, Arnie! Don't keep us waiting!"

Methodically, Dortmunder scooped the jewelry back into the plastic bag. Standing, he put the plastic bag in his jacket pocket and, as Arnie opened the door to the cops, Dortmunder stepped into the bedroom (girlie calendars, from gas stations and coal companies). Behind him, Arnie was saying, "What now?"

"Just a little chat, Arnie. You alone?"

"I'm always alone. Do I know you? You're Flynn, aren't you? Who's this guy?"

"This is Officer Rashab, Arnie. You happen to have any stolen goods in your possession?"

"No. You happen to have a search warrant in yours?"

"Would we need one, Arnie?"

There was no fire escape outside this room. Dortmunder pressed his forehead against the window, looked down, and saw it was no good.

"You guys'll do what you wanna do anyway. You've tossed this place yourself before, you know that. And all you ever got was dirty socks."

"Maybe we'll be luckier this time."

"Depends how you feel about dirty socks."

Dortmunder stepped into the bathroom. (Horse-print and hunting-scene calendars.) No window, only a small exhaust grid. Dortmunder sighed and stepped back into the bedroom.

"I got enough dirty socks of my own, Arnie. Get into your coat."

"I'm going somewhere?"

"We're having a party."

Dortmunder stepped into the closet. (Aubrey Beardsley calendars.) It smelled very badly of dirty socks. He pushed through the coats and pants and sweaters and pressed his back against the wall. The voices came closer.

"I went to a party once. They made me go home after twenty minutes."

"Maybe that'll happen this time, too."

The closet door opened. Arnie, disgusted, looked past coat shoulders at Dortmunder's eyes. "My friends," he said.

Behind him, the talking cop said, "What's that?"

"You're my friends," Arnie said, taking a coat out of the closet. "You're my only friends in the world." He shut the closet door.

"We take an interest in you," said the talking cop.

The voices receded. The front door slammed. Dortmunder sighed, which he immediately regretted, because it involved taking a deep breath full of dirty socks. He opened the closet door, leaned out, breathed, and listened. Not a sound. He left the closet, shaking his head, and went back into the living room.

All alone. And the funny thing was, the cops seemed to have picked Arnie up just for the hell of it. "Hmmm," Dortmunder said.

There was a phone on the end table beside the sofa. Dortmunder sat down there, said, "Stoon," and dialed Andy Kelp's number. "If I get that machine . . ."

The phone rang twice and a girl answered: "Hello?" She sounded young and pretty. All girls who sound young sound pretty, which has led to some unfortunate later discoveries in this life.

Dortmunder said, "Uhhh— Is Andy there?"

"Who?"

"Did I dial wrong? I'm looking for Andy Kelp."

"No, I'm sorry, I— Oh!"

"Oh?"

"You mean *Andy!*"

So it wasn't a wrong number, it was a dummy. Here was this girl in Kelp's apartment, answering Kelp's phone, and it was taking her a long long time to realize the call was for Kelp. "That's right," Dortmunder said. "I mean Andy."

"Oh, I guess he didn't turn it off," she said.

Then Dortmunder knew. He didn't know what, exactly, not yet, but in a general sort of way he *knew.* And it wasn't this girl's fault, it was Kelp's fault. Naturally. Apologizing to the girl in his head for his previous bad thoughts about her, he said, "Didn't turn what off?"

"See, I just met Andy last night," she said. "In a bar. My name's Sherri?"

"Aren't you sure?"

"Sure I'm sure. Anyway, Andy told me about all these wonderful telephone gadgets he had, and we went to his place and he showed them to me, and then he said he'd show me the phone-ahead gadget. So he put this little box on his phone, all set up with my home phone number, and then we came over here to my place to wait for somebody to call him, because then it would ring here instead of there, and he wouldn't miss any calls."

"Uh-huh."

"But nobody ever called."

"That's a shame," said Dortmunder.

"Yeah, isn't it? So then he left this morning, but I guess he forgot to take the box off his phone when he got home."

"He called me this morning."

"I guess he can call out, but if you call in it gets transferred here."

"You live near him?"

"Oh, no, I'm way over here on the East Side. Near the Queensboro Bridge."

"Ah," said Dortmunder. "And any time I happen to dial Andy Kelp's phone number, *his* phone won't ring, but yours will, way over there by the Queensboro Bridge."

"Gee, I guess that's right."

"He probably won't hear that phone of yours when it rings, will he? Not even if you open your windows."

"Oh, no, he couldn't possibly."

"That's what I figured," Dortmunder said. Very very gently, he hung up.

10

Chief Inspector Francis Xavier Mologna (pronounced Maloney) of the New York City Police Department and Agent
Malcolm Zachary of the Federal Bureau of Investigation
loved one another imperfectly. They were of course on the
same side in the war between the forces of order and the
forces of disorder, and they would of course cooperate fully
with one another whenever that war might find them both
engaged on the same field of battle, and they did of course
deeply admire one another's branch of service in this war as
well as respect one another individually as long-term profes-
sionals. Apart from which, each thought the other was an
asshole.

"The man's an asshole," Mologna told Leon, his nigger
faggot secretary, when the latter entered the former's office to
announce the arrival of the aforesaid.

"A reigning asshole," Leon agreed. "But he's in my office
and he'd rather be in yours, and I too would rather he was in
yours."

"A rainin asshole? Is that one of your disgustin faggot
perversions?"

"Yes," said Leon. "Shall I send him in?"

"If he's still there," Mologna said hopefully.

He was still there. In fact, at that very instant, in the
outer office, Agent Zachary was saying, "The man's an asshole, Bob," to his partner, Freedly.

"But still we have to cooperate with him, Mac," Freedly
said.

"*I* know that. I just want to go on record with you, off
the record, that the man's an asshole."

"Agreed."

Leon opened the connecting door, smiled coquettishly at
the two FBI men, and said, "Inspector Mologna will see you
now."

At his desk Mologna grumbled, "I'll *never* be able to see

that asshole," then smiled and heaved to his feet and presented his hand and his beer belly and his beaming face in the direction of Zachary and Freedly as they entered. Hands were shaken as Leon exited, shutting the door.

Zachary gestured at the windows behind Mologna's desk. "Magnificent view."

It was. "Yes, it is," Mologna said.

"Brooklyn Bridge, isn't it?"

It was. "Yes, it is," Mologna said.

So much for small talk. Zachary took one of the brown leather chairs facing the desk (Freedly took the other) and said, "So far as we can tell, the Greeks don't have it."

"Of course they don't," Mologna said, dropping back into his padded high-back swivel chair. "I said so this mornin. Hold on just a minute." And he pressed a button on his intercom, then looked at the door.

Which opened. Leon said, "You want me?"

"You might as well take notes."

"I'll get my little pad."

Zachary and Freedly exchanged a glance. There was something funny about that secretary.

Leon entered, shut the door, sashayed to his little chair in the corner, prettily crossed his legs, perched his notebook on the upper knee, poised his pen, and looked expectantly at everybody.

"As I was sayin," Mologna said (Leon did quick squiggly shorthand), "I said this mornin—"

Zachary said, "You'll copy to me, won't you?"

"—the— What?"

Zachary nodded at Leon. "The notes of the meeting."

"Certainly. Leon? Copy for the FBI."

"Oh, absolutely," Leon said.

Leon and Mologna exchanged a glance.

Zachary and Freedly exchanged a glance.

Mologna said, "*As* I was sayin, I said this mornin this ruby ring wasn't taken by any of your foreign political types. It's—"

"That appears," Zachary said, "to be true at least in the case of the Greek Cypriot underground. We have good penetration in most of their organizations, and the word to us is, they don't have it."

"That's what I've been sayin."

"Which leaves the Turks and the Russians."

"And the Armenians," Freedly added.

"Thank you, Bob, you're absolutely right."

"It also leaves," Mologna said, "a nice homegrown burglar, ancestry as yet undetermined."

"Of course," Zachary said, "there is always that possibility. At the Bureau—and I've discussed this now with sog—and our feeling—"

Mologna said, "Sog?"

"Seat of Government," Zachary explained. "That's what we call the main Bureau headquarters in Washington."

"Seat of Government," Mologna echoed. He and Leon exchanged a glance.

"Abbreviated, S, O, G, pronounced sog. And our feeling is, the likelihood still remains upmost for a politically motivated removal."

"Theft."

"Technically, of course, it is a theft."

"With a thief," Mologna said.

"Frankly," Zachary said, "I hope—and I'm sure the Bureau hopes—you turn out to be right."

"All the fellas down there at sog."

Zachary frowned a bit. Was Mologna being sardonic? It didn't seem possible, from a man with such a bad Long Island accent and such a big, big stomach. "That's right," he said. "And it would be much simpler and easier if in fact it is merely a domestic burglar. One of our problems otherwise is diplomatic immunity."

"Diplomatic immunity?" Mologna shook his head, his expression determined. "This isn't some parkin ticket, man. There's no immunity from grand larceny."

Zachary and Freedly exchanged a glance. Zachary explained, "Most of these organizations—terrorist groups, nationalist cells, rebel conclaves—have linkages to one or another standing government. Which gives them access to diplomatic pouches. Baggage leaving any of the various UN missions or the foreign consulates and embassies here in New York and in Washington, it all goes through unchecked and unsearched. *That's* the diplomatic immunity I'm talking about. Anything at all can go in or out of this country in a diplomatic pouch and no one the wiser."

"We're very lucky," Freedly added, "that the original group involved in the raid at the airport had already been disavowed by the Greek government, forcing them to find an alternate method for smuggling the ring out of the country."

"And you're also lucky," Mologna told him, "that what we're lookin for this time is just some local hooligan."

"We'd prefer to be that fortunate," Zachary agreed. "Do you have any hard evidence at the moment to support your theory?"

"Hard evidence? That bit of wire bypassin the alarm box, how's that for evidence? The door bein jimmied that—"

"Yes, yes," Zachary said, raising a hand to stem the flow. "I remember all that from the meeting this morning. I meant since then."

Mologna and Leon exchanged a glance. Mologna said, "It's been at best two hours since that meetin. We're good, Mr. Zachary, but nobody's *that* good."

Zachary and Freedly exchanged a glance. Zachary said, "But you have taken steps."

"Of course I've taken steps. We're talkin to our informants, we're arrestin every known criminal in the five boroughs, we're puttin pressure on the entire underworld." Mologna nodded in self-satisfaction. "It won't take long. We'll get results."

"How soon, do you suppose? If you're right, that is."

"If I'm right?" Mologna and Leon exchanged a glance. "Two days, three days. I'll keep you informed of progress."

"Thank you. Meantime, we'll pursue the alternate theory that the ring's disappearance has a political basis, and of course we'll be delighted to keep you informed of *our* progress."

Mologna and Leon exchanged a glance. Mologna said, "Progress. On the international front."

Zachary and Freedly exchanged a glance. Zachary said, "Yes. On the international front."

"The Armenians," Freedly added, "are looking particularly interesting."

Mologna looked particularly interested. "Are they, now?"

Zachary nodded. "Bob's right," he said. "Nationalists without a current nation do tend to go to extremes. The Moluccans, for instance. Palestinians."

"Puerto Ricans," added Freedly.

"To an extent," agreed Zachary.

Mologna and Leon exchanged a glance.

Zachary got to his feet. (Freedly followed suit.) "Interagency cooperation," Zachary said, "is so important in a matter like this."

Mologna heaved to his feet, resting his beer belly on the desktop. "We couldn't possibly succeed without it," he said. "I'm very happy to have you fellows aboard in this little burglary case."

"We feel the same way," Zachary assured him. "In such a delicate international affair, we're delighted to have such able and willing cooperation at the local level."

Hands were shaken. Leon drew a little caricature of Freedly, wearing pendant earrings. The federal agents made their departure, closing the door behind themselves.

"The man's an asshole," Zachary and Mologna said to Freedly and Leon.

11

Dortmunder brought home a Whopper from the Burger King, opened a can of beer, and started phoning around. The first several guys he called weren't home. Then he reached one fellow's wife, who said, "Jack's in jail."

"In jail? Since when?"

"Since about half an hour ago. I just put the soufflé in the oven and in walk these cops. So much for lunch."

"Wha'd they grab him for?"

"Practice. Took him in for questioning, is all. They don't have a thing on him and they know it."

"So they'll have to let him go."

"Sure. And here I am with cold, soggy soufflé. It's just harassment, that's all."

"Listen," Dortmunder said. "What I wanted to ask Jack is, does he know the address of a fellow called Stoon. Would you maybe know it?"

"Stoon? Oh, I think I know who you mean, but I don't know where he lives."

"Oh. Okay."

"Sorry."

"Tsokay. Sorry about Jack."

"It's the soufflé I feel sorry for."

The next two guys weren't home, but the one after that was. He was home, and he was mad. "I just been to the precinct," he said. "They had me there two hours."

"For what?"

"Questioning, they call it. Bullshit is what *I* call it. They're grabbing people all over the city."

"What is it, a stunt?"

"No, it's that ruby, the one got knocked over out to Kennedy last night. That's what they're looking for, and they're squeezing hard. I never seen nothing like it."

"It's real valuable, huh?"

"I don't know, Dortmunder, I don't think that's it. Valuable things get stolen, am I right? That's what they're for. I mean, it happens a lot. I mean, you wouldn't go out to steal apple cores."

"So what's the point?"

"Beats me. This ruby's *important* somehow. It's got the law very agitated."

"It'll blow over," Dortmunder said. "What I'm calling about, do you know a guy named Stoon?"

"Stoon. Yeah."

"Do you have an address?"

"On Perry Street, in the Village. Twenty-one, I think, maybe twenty-three. His name's on the bell."

"Thanks."

"I'll tell you one thing. I'm glad I'm not the guy boosted that ruby. The heat is *intense*."

"I know what you mean," Dortmunder said.

Next, he tried Kelp's number again, just in case the idiot had retired his phone-ahead box, but it was the cheery girl who answered. "Oh," Dortmunder said. "He's still got that box on, huh? Sorry to bother you."

"No," said the girl, "I'm here—" But Dortmunder, disgusted, was already hanging up, breaking the connection before she said, "—at Andy's apartment."

Immediately, with Dortmunder's hand still on it, the phone rang. He picked up the receiver again: "Hello?"

"You been on the phone."

"I'm still on the phone," Dortmunder pointed out. "How you doing, Stan?"

"I'm okay," Stan Murch said. "I think I got a nice one. Needs some planning, some leadership. You available?"

"Very," Dortmunder said.

"I thought, just a couple guys. Ralph Winslow, you know him?"

"Sure. He's okay."

"And Tiny Bulcher."

"Is he out again?"

"Turned out the gorilla didn't press charges."

"Oh."

"We'll meet tonight at the O.J. Ten o'clock good?"

"Sure."

"Do you know how I can get in touch with Andy Kelp?"

"No," said Dortmunder.

12

The name "Stoon" appeared among the doorbells at neither 21 nor 23 Perry Street. Coming out of the latter, pausing on the stoop to consider the perfidy of life, Dortmunder saw activity diagonally across the way. Three men were emerging from a building over there, the two flankers each holding an elbow of the one in the middle. Additionally, the flanker on the left was carrying a large blue canvas bag, which appeared to be very heavy. The three men hustled across the street to a battered light blue Ford parked near Dortmunder, who could see that the man in the middle—short, round-faced—seemed much less happy than his companions, both of whom were large, rather beefy, and obviously quite pleased with themselves. As they stuffed their short companion into the back seat of the Ford and the heavy blue canvas bag into the front seat, one of them said, "This'll keep *you* inside for quite a while." What the short man answered, if anything, Dortmunder didn't hear.

The two big, self-satisfied men also entered the Ford, one in front and one in back, and the car drove away. Dortmunder watched it go. At the corner, it turned and drove out of sight.

Dortmunder sighed. There was no question in his mind, of course, but he might as well make absolutely sure. He walked across the street, entered the vestibule of the building the trio had appeared from, and scanned the names beside the bells.

Stoon.

"You lookin for somebody?"

Dortmunder turned and saw a truculent fortyish Puerto Rican armed with a push broom. The super. Dortmunder said, "Liebowitz."

"They moved out," the super said.

"Oh."

Dortmunder walked away. At the corner, a cop looked at

him very hard. By then Dortmunder was so disgusted that, forgetting the plastic bag of jewelry in his jacket pocket, he looked back at the cop just as hard. The cop shrugged and went on about his business.

Dortmunder went home.

13

Jack Mackenzie got along so well with the cops because they all thought he was Irish. His ancestry was, in fact, Scottish, a shameful secret wild horses couldn't have dragged out of him.

Being a police reporter for a large metropolitan TV station, it was a good thing Mackenzie was so tight with the men in blue—otherwise, he wouldn't have kept the job very long. But the cops knew good old Jack would always get their names right, would put them on camera if at all possible, would always believe their version of how the suspect fell off the roof, and would never twit them for their occasional inevitable failures. And that's why, when Chief Inspector Francis Xavier Mologna (which Jack Mackenzie *always* pronounced Maloney) decided to go public with this Byzantine Fire problem, it was red-haired, freckle-faced, jovial, hard-drinking, pseudo-Irish Jack Mackenzie who got the nod for the exclusive interview.

The meeting took place in a conference room at Headquarters, down several flights from Mologna's own office. With its indirect lighting, serious-looking desk, and windowless walls thoroughly diapered in sound-absorbing Virgin-Mary-blue drapes, this room had been designed for television. If a police spokesman stood behind that desk, in front of those drapes, holding up an old .22 rifle while announcing that the arrest of those four college sophomores had just narrowly averted the overthrow of the Republic, you *believed* him.

The meeting was scheduled at four o'clock, just early

enough to make the opening segment of the six o'clock news. (The rest of the press would get the story a bit later, also in time for the six o'clock news, but not till the end of the program rather than the beginning. Friendship is a wonderful thing.) Mackenzie arrived a bit early accompanied by his three-man crew (one operated the camera, one ran the sound equipment, and the union wouldn't tell anybody what the third man did), and he joshed with the officer on guard in the hallway while his boys set up their equipment and checked light levels over every square inch of the room.

Mologna himself, in a uniform so rich with braid that he looked like an ocean liner at night, emerged from the elevator down the hall at three minutes past four, accompanied by his secretary, Sergeant Leon Windrift, and two anonymous plainclothes detectives carrying folders full of handouts and statistics. Mologna and Mackenzie met in the hall and shook hands, beaming with approval on one another. "Good to see you, Jack," said Mologna.

"How are you, Chief Inspector? You're looking fine. Lost a couple pounds, didn't you?"

In fact, Mologna had gained a few pounds. His smile even broader and happier than before, he patted his beer belly—*thup, thup*—and said, "Hard to keep in fightin trim, stuck to that desk every day."

"Well, you're looking fine," Mackenzie repeated, which was about as far as he could take such nonsense.

The two went on into the conference room, followed by Mologna's minions, and Mackenzie's crew put out their cigarettes and prepared to go to work. Since this was to be an interview rather than a press conference—that was scheduled at four-thirty, in this same room—Mologna sat at the desk rather than stand behind it (his beer belly hardly showed at all), while Mackenzie took the chair to the right of the desk. More light level readings were taken, and then the sound man asked them to just talk to one another while he took sound levels. Both participants were old hands at this and chatted about baseball—the new season just getting under way down there in Florida, if Mackenzie were a sports re-

porter he could be down there now in the warm, etc., etc.—
until the sound man told them they could stop the drivel.
Then they settled down to the business at hand.

Mackenzie: "Maybe you better give me my lead-in question. I'm not sure exactly what you want to announce here."

Mologna: "I want to announce progress on this fuckin
ruby ring. Why not tell me you understand I'm in charge and
how'm I doin?"

Mackenzie: "Okay, fine. Chief Inspector Mologna,
you've been placed in charge of the investigation into last
night's theft of the Byzantine Fire. Do you have any progress
to report?"

Mologna: "Well, yes and no, Jack. We have the bunch
that pulled the job out at Kennedy International Airport, but
unfortunately we don't as yet have the ring."

Mackenzie: "But arrests have been made?"

Mologna: "Definitely. We've held back the announcement, hopin to finish the case. The alleged perpetrators are
aliens, apparently involved in the current troubles in Cyprus.
We nabbed all four this mornin."

Mackenzie: "So the theft of the Byzantine Fire was a
political act."

Mologna (*chuckles*): "Well, Jack, that may be the way *they*
look at it. I'm a simple New York cop, and to me a holdup is a
holdup."

Mackenzie: "So these people will be tried like any common criminal."

Mologna: "That's up to the courts, Jack."

Mackenzie: "Yes, of course. Chief Inspector, if you are
satisfied you have in fact apprehended the criminals, why is it
the Byzantine Fire is still missing?"

Mologna: "Well, Jack, that's the reason I want to make a
direct appeal to the public. The fact is, and this is why we've
made no announcement till now, the ring was stolen *twice*."

Mackenzie: "Twice?"

Mologna: "That's right, Jack. The original perpetrators
intended to smuggle the ring out of the country, and in connection with their plans they left it in a jeweler's shop on

Rockaway Boulevard in the South Ozone Park section of Queens."

Mackenzie: "Off the tape here, do you have a color photo of this store? Otherwise I'll have to phone our people to get out there right away."

Mologna: "Now, Jack, you know I take care of you. Turnbull here has everythin you need."

Mackenzie: "Great. Back on the tape. Chief Inspector, you say the ring was left in a jeweler's shop?"

Mologna: "That's right, Jack. Due to some very good police work—and I want to say that the Federal Bureau of Investigation was very helpful in this part of the case—we'd rounded up the entire gang well before sunup this mornin. Unfortunately, durin that time the jeweler's shop underwent an entirely unconnected burglary. Some thief, as yet unapprehended, took away the Byzantine Fire along with the rest of his loot from the store. *This* is the man we are now lookin for."

Mackenzie: "Chief Inspector, do you mean to say that some minor-league crook in this city is now in possession of the multi-million-dollar Byzantine Fire?"

Mologna: "That's precisely the case, Jack."

Mackenzie: "Chief Inspector, may I ask what is being done?"

Mologna: "Everythin is bein done, Jack. Since the discovery of the burglary, I have put into effect an order to question every known criminal in the city of New York."

Mackenzie: "A pretty large order, Chief Inspector."

Mologna: "We're devotin our full resources to the job, Jack." (Out of camera range, Sergeant Leon Windrift slid a piece of paper onto the desk in front of Mologna, who did not blatantly look at it.) "As of three o'clock this afternoon, in all five boroughs of this city, seventeen thousand, three hundred and fifty-four individuals have been picked up for questionin. The result so far of this blitz has been six hundred and ninety-one arrests for crimes and offenses unrelated to the disappearance of the Byzantine Fire."

Mackenzie: "Chief Inspector, are you saying that so far

today six hundred ninety-one unsolved crimes have been solved?"

Mologna: "That's up to the courts, Jack. All I can tell you is, *we're* satisfied with the results up till now."

Mackenzie: "So, no matter what else happens, today's police blitz has been a definite plus from the point of view of the honest citizens of New York."

Mologna: "I'd say so, Jack. But now we'd like to ask those honest citizens to give us their assistance." (*turning directly to camera*) "The Byzantine Fire is a very valuable ruby ring, but it's more than that. As Americans, we were makin a gift of that ruby ring, all of us, to a friendly nation. As New Yorkers, I think we all feel a little ashamed that this has happened in our fair city. I am showin you a picture of the Byzantine Fire. If you have seen this ring, or if you have any information at all that could be helpful in this investigation, please call the special police number you now see on your screen." (*turns back to Mackenzie*)

Mackenzie: "And in the meantime, Chief Inspector, the police blitz will continue?"

Mologna: "Absolutely, Jack."

Mackenzie: "Until the Byzantine Fire is found."

Mologna: "Jack, the criminal element in the city of New York will learn to regret the very existence of the Byzantine Fire."

Mackenzie: "Thank you very much, Chief Inspector Francis Mologna."

That ended the interview. Mackenzie and Mologna shook hands once more and exchanged a few words while Mackenzie's crew packed up. Then Mologna resat behind the desk to await the rest of the press—due now to arrive in about ten minutes—while Mackenzie hurried back to the TV station, there to pose against another Virgin-Mary-blue drape for reaction shots and a lead-in explanation of the story and better-organized phrasing of a couple of his questions. These shots were mixed with portions of the interview tape, plus a nice clear color photo of the facade of Skoukakis Credit Jewelers, plus another nice clear color photo of the Byzantine Fire

on a background of black velvet, plus a superimposition of
the special police number (which would be dialed by a lot of
giggling 12-year-olds), and the whole thing was ready just in
time for the six o'clock news.

A very attractive little scoop.

14

It's a pity Dortmunder watched the wrong channel. At six-oh-
three, while Jack Mackenzie was describing Dortmunder's
most recent exploit (anonymously) to several hundred thousand more or less indifferent viewers, his potentially most rapt
audience was a bare few clicks away along the dial, watching
something called "file film" of people in white dresses running
around a sunny broad tree-lined street amid the pop-chatter
of small arms fire, as a voice-over announcer stated that fighting between government troops and rebels had broken out yet
again. *Where* this fighting had broken out Dortmunder wasn't
sure, not having paid that close attention to the voice-over
voice. On the other hand, he didn't much care, either; if a lot
of people in white dresses wanted to run around a sunny
broad tree-lined street while being shot at, that was up to
them. Dortmunder was mostly brooding about his own problems: drinking beer, paying minimal attention to the six
o'clock news, and brooding.

May came home while the sports news was being given
its usual exhaustive airing, a subject in which Dortmunder's
lack of interest was so profound that he hadn't waited until
the commercial to go get another beer. Returning to the living room with the new beer, he saw May walk in the front
door and switched off the TV set just as the post-sports commercial was starting. Which was also unfortunate, because
right after *that* commercial the hot news about the Byzantine
Fire was going to be broadcast by the (helplessly furious at

both Mackenzie and Mologna) police beat reporter for this channel, a man blamelessly suffering because his Irish name—Costello—sounded Italian.

"Let me take one of those," Dortmunder said, and took her left-hand grocery sack.

"Thanks." The cigarette bobbled in the corner of her mouth.

It was May's belief that her activities as a cashier down at the Safeway made her in a way a member of the Safeway family, and how could the family begrudge her a little for herself? So every day she came home with a couple of full grocery sacks, which was very helpful for their domestic economy.

They carried today's groceries to the kitchen, with May saying along the way, "Somebody's passing fake food stamps."

"Counterfeit?"

"It's the noncash economy you read about," May said. "Credit cards, checks, food stamps. People don't deal in money any more."

"Um," said Dortmunder. The noncash economy was one of his major career problems. No cash payrolls, no cash deliveries, no cash anywhere.

"They're nice, too," May said. "Very good plates. The only trouble is, the paper's different. Thinner. You can feel the difference."

"Not smart," Dortmunder said.

"That's right. Does a cashier look at all that paper? No. But you *touch* every piece that comes by."

"Food stamps." Dortmunder leaned against the sink, slurping at his beer while May put the groceries away. "You wouldn't think it'd be worth it."

"Oh, no? With prices the way they are? You just don't know, John."

"I guess not."

"If I didn't have the job at the Safeway, I wouldn't mind some queer food stamps myself."

"Big operation," Dortmunder mused. "You've got your

printer, you've got your salesmen on the street."

"I was thinking," May said. "I could maybe be a sales-man. Right there at the register."

Dortmunder frowned at her. "I don't know, May. I wouldn't like you to take chances."

"Just to deal with customers I know. I'll think about it, anyway."

"It'd be an easy pinch, is all."

"I won't do it unless things get really tight around here. How'd you do with Arnie?"

"Um," Dortmunder said.

May was putting two plastic-wrapped trays of chicken parts in the refrigerator. She gave Dortmunder a questioning look, closed the refrigerator door, and while folding up the grocery sacks said, "Something went wrong."

"Arnie got arrested. While I was there."

"They didn't take you with?"

"They didn't see me."

"That's good. Wha'd they take him for?"

"It's a sweep. There was some big jewel robbery out at Kennedy last night."

"I saw something about it in the paper."

"So the law's busting everybody," Dortmunder said, "looking for it."

"The poor guy."

"That took it?" Dortmunder shook his head. "He de-serves what he gets, making all this trouble. It's the guys like Arnie I feel sorry for. Arnie and me."

"Won't they have to let him go after a while?"

"Arnie's probably out already," Dortmunder said, "but he won't be buying for a while. And I heard about another possible guy and went there, and the cops were grabbing him, too. I guess they're hitting particular on the fences because it's a jewel."

"So you've still got the goods?"

"In the bedroom."

May would know he meant the hiding place in the back of the dresser. "Never mind," she said. "You'll have better luck tomorrow." Fishing out a new cigarette, she lit it from the final coal of the old one, then flipped the ember into the sink, where it briefly sizzled.

"I'm sorry, May," Dortmunder said.

"It's not your fault," she said. "Besides, you never know what's going to happen in this life. That's why I brought home the chicken. We'll eat out tomorrow."

"Sure." As much to encourage himself as her, he said, "Stan Murch called. He's got something, he says. Needs a planner."

"Well, that's you."

"I'm seeing him tonight."

"What's the score?"

"I don't know yet," Dortmunder said. "I hope it isn't jewelry again."

"The noncash economy," May said, smiling.

"Maybe it's food stamps," Dortmunder said.

15

When Malcolm Zachary got mad, he got mad like an FBI man. His jaw clenched so four-square and rock-hard he looked like Dick Tracy. His shoulders became absolutely straight and right-angled and level with the floor, as though he were wearing a cardboard box from the liquor store under his coat. His eyes became very intense, like Superman looking through walls. And when he spoke, little muscle bunches in his cheeks did tangos beneath the skin: "Mo-*log*-na," he said, slowly and deliberately. "Mo-*log*-na, Mo-*log*-na, Mo-*log*-na."

"I couldn't agree more, Mac," said Freedly, whose manner when enraged was exactly the reverse. Freedly's eyebrows and moustache and shoulders became all slumped and rounded, as though gravity were overcoming him, and he got the look in his eye of a man trying to figure out how to get even. Which he was.

Zachary and Freedly had also failed to watch the right

TV news at six o'clock, or in fact any news at all, because
they were in conference at that time with Harry Cabot, their
liaison from the CIA, a smooth fiftyish man with a distin-
guished handsomeness and an air of knowing more than he
was saying. Fresh from suborning an overly enlightened Central American government, Cabot had been rewarded for a
dirty job well done by being given this soft assignment in
New York: funneling to the FBI some of the CIA's data on
various foreign insurgent groups potentially involved with the
Byzantine Fire. He was, in fact, just speaking about the Armenians, in an amused and dismissive but not entirely com-
prehensible manner, when the phone rang in Zachary and
Freedly's small office here on East 69th Street, and the blow
fell: Chief Inspector Mologna had given a statement to the
press.

"Harry, we're going to have to look at this," Zachary
said. He had white spots beside his nose and the general air of
a man whose parachute doesn't seem to be opening.

"I'll come with you," Cabot said.

So the three of them went down to the monitor room,
where news programs were watched and taped, and the tape
of the Mackenzie-Mologna interview was run for them, and
that's when Zachary's jaw became very square and Freedly's
moustache became very drooped.

The part that galled the most was where Mologna
thanked the FBI for its assistance in "rounding up" the jeweler Skoukakis and the arrested Cypriots, implying very
clearly that it was the New York Police Department which
had done the lion's share of the said rounding up. "They
weren't even *in* the case!" Zachary cried. "They've *never* been
in the case! Running around after second-story men!"

They watched the tape to the end, then watched it
through a second time, and in the ensuing silence Freedly
said, thoughtfully, "Has he blown security, Mac? Do we have
a complaint over his head, to the Commissioner?"

Zachary thought about that for a second or two, then
reluctantly shook his head. "There was no lid clamped," he
said. "We naturally assumed we were all gentlemen, that's all;

we'd agree on a joint announcement at the proper time." (In fact, Zachary had been planning a unilateral announcement of his own late tomorrow morning—being federal, he naturally thought in terms of the national media, requiring an earlier deadline—and part of his rage was at Mologna having stolen a march on him.) "Let's go back upstairs," he said, lunging to his feet like an angry FBI man. He thanked the monitor room technicians in a curt but manly way, and they left.

In the elevator Freedly, still casting about for revenge, said, "Well, has he hampered our investigation?"

"Of course he has! The son of a bitch."

"Well, then."

The elevator door opened and they headed down the corridor. Harry Cabot said, "If I were Chief Inspector Mologna—" (he pronounced it right) "—and I were charged with hampering your investigation, I would point out that you people are concentrating on foreign nationalist groups. By publicly stating that the investigation is aimed at domestic thieves, I have lulled your actual suspects and therefore *aided* your investigation."

"Shit," said Zachary.

"Ditto," said Freedly.

Back in the office, Zachary sat at his desk while Freedly and Cabot shared the sofa. Zachary said, "When we turn up the ring, Bob, when we rub Mo-log-na's nose in it that it *wasn't* one of his hole-in-corner little burglars, we'll have our own little press conference."

Freedly made no response. He merely sat there, a very dubious look on his face. Zachary said, "Bob?"

"Yes, Mac?"

"*You* don't think it was just a burglar, do you?"

"Mac," Freedly said, with obvious reluctance, "I'm not sure."

"Oh, *Bob!*" Zachary said, in a tone of utter betrayal.

"It wasn't the Greeks," Freedly said. "According to Harry here, it's looking more and more like it wasn't the dissident Turks. It's pretty surely not the Armenians."

"There's still the Bulgarians," Zachary said.

"Ye-ess."

"And our friends of the KGB. And the Serbo-Croats. And it still *could* be the Turks. Couldn't it, Harry?"

Cabot nodded, more in amusement than agreement. "The Turks are still a possibility," he said. "Remote, but possible."

"Hell, Bob," Zachary said, "there's groups out there we haven't even thought about yet. What about the Kurds?"

Freedly looked astonished. "The Kurds? What've *they* got to do with the Byzantine Fire?"

"They've been in opposition to Turkey a long time."

Cabot cleared his throat. "For the last thirty years," he gently pointed out, "the Kurds' main revolt has been against Iran."

"Well, how about Iran?" Zachary looked around like a hungry bird. "Iran," he repeated. "They poke their nose into just about everything in that Black Sea area. Particularly with the Shah out and the religious nuts in."

Freedly said, "Mac, there hasn't been the slightest rumble from Iran. If there was, Harry would know about it."

"That's true," Cabot said.

"Irani insurgents, then."

Agreeably, Cabot said, "Another possibility, of course, though rather remote." Seeing that Zachary was about to ring in yet another nation or band of dissidents, Cabot raised a restraining hand and said, "Still, the point has been adequately made. We are nowhere near the end of potential foreign suspects. When this unfortunate news in re Inspector Mologna arrived, however, I was just finishing my discussion of the more likely of these groups, and I'd intended to segue to another and perhaps equally important topic."

Zachary restrained himself with the greatest difficulty. He bubbled with undeclared Kazaks, Circassians, Uzbeks, Albanians, Lebanese, and Cypriot Maronites, all of whom made him mutely fidget and squirm at his desk, picking up pencils and paperweights, then putting them down again.

Having bludgeoned the previous conversation to death

with practiced civility, Cabot said, "Whichever of our Free World allies turns out to be responsible for this theft, if any, the fact is that just about every group we've mentioned, and some we haven't discussed as yet, has become active *since* the theft. So far, we know of the entrance into this country in the last twenty-four hours of a Turkish Secret Police assassination team, a Greek Army counterinsurgency guerrilla squad, members of two separate Cypriot Greek nationalist movements (who may spend all their time here gunning for one another and therefore fail to become a substantive factor from our point of view), two officers of the Bulgarian External Police, a KGB operative with deep connections to the Cypriot Turk nationalist movement, and a Lebanese Christian assassin. There is also the rumored arrival via Montreal of two members of the Smyrna Schism, religious fanatics who broke away from the Russian Orthodox Church in the late seventeen hundreds and live in catacombs under Smyrna. They are rumored to favor the beheading of heretics. In addition, various embassies in Washington—the Turkish, Greek, Russian, Yugoslav, Lebanese, some others—have requested official briefings on the matter. At the UN, the British have called for—"

"The British!" Surprise unsealed Zachary's lips. "What've *they* got to do with it?"

"The British take a proprietary interest in the entire planet," Cabot told him. "They think of themselves as our landlords, and they have called for a United Nations fact-finding team to assist the rest of us in our investigations. They have also volunteered to lead this fact-finding team themselves."

"Good of them," Zachary said.

"But the main problem right now," Cabot said, "aside from the loss of the ring itself, of course, is all these foreign gunmen running around New York, hunting the ring and one another. This theft is enough of an international incident as it is; Washington would be *very* displeased if New York were turned into another Beirut, with shooting in the streets."

"New York would be displeased, too," Freedly said.

"No doubt," agreed Cabot.

Acidly, Zachary said, "Mo-log-na could give another press conference."

Unexpectedly, Cabot chuckled. The other two, seeing nothing amusing anywhere in the visible landscape, looked at him with annoyed surprise. "I'm sorry," Cabot said. "I was just thinking, what if Inspector Mologna were right? What if some passing burglar, uninterested in Cyprus or Turkey or NATO or the Russian Orthodox Church or *any* of it, just happened to pick up the Byzantine Fire in the course of his normal operations? And now the world is filling up with police forces, intelligence agencies, guerrilla bands, assassination teams, religious fanatics, all pointed at that poor bastard's head." With another chuckle, Cabot said, "I wouldn't want to be him."

"I wish Mo-log-na was him," Zachary said.

16

Dortmunder had deliberately taken a subway in the wrong direction from Times Square to get away from a pair of uniformed cops who had been gazing at him with steadily increasing interest, so it was a quarter after ten, fifteen minutes late, before he walked into the O. J. Bar and Grill on Amsterdam Avenue, where three of the regulars were discussing Cyprus—probably because it was in the news in connection with the Byzantine Fire. "All you gotta do is look onna map," one of the regulars was saying. "Cyprus is right there by Turkey. Greece is way to hell and gone."

"Oh, yeah?" said the second regular. "You happen to be a Turk, by any chance?"

"I happen," the first regular said, with a dangerous glint in his eye, "to be Polish and Norwegian. You got any objections?"

"Well, *I* happen," said the second regular, "to be one

hunnerd percent Greek, and I'm here to tell you *you* happen to be fulla shit. Both the Polish part and the Norwegian part. Both parts, fulla shit."

"Wait a minute, fellas," said the third regular. "Let's not cast a lotta national aspersions."

"I'm not casting anything," said the second regular. "This Norwegian Polack's telling *me* where Greece is."

"What is this?" demanded the first regular. "You have to be Greek before you know where Greece is?"

"There's something in what he says," said the third regular, who apparently saw himself as the voice of reason in a world of extremes.

"There's horseshit in what he says," said the second regular.

Dortmunder approached the bar some distance from the nationalists, where Rollo the bartender, tall, meaty, balding, blue-jawed, wearing a dirty white shirt and a dirty white apron, stood looking up at the color TV set, on which at that moment several very clean people were pretending to look worried in a very clean hospital room. "Whadaya say," said Dortmunder.

Rollo looked down from the screen. "Now they're rerunning the made-for-TV movies," he said, "and claiming they're movies. It's Whatsisname's law."

"It's what?"

"You know," Rollo said. "That law. Where the bad shit drives out the good."

"The good shit?" It occurred to Dortmunder that Rollo was beginning to sound like one of his own customers. Maybe he'd been in this job too long.

"Just a minute," Rollo said, and walked away to where the nationalists were beginning to threaten incursions into one another's territory. "You boys wanna fight," Rollo said, "you go home and fight with your wives. You wanna drink beer, you come here."

The pro-Turk Norwegian Pole said, "Exactly. That's what I come here for. I'm disinterested. I'm not even Turkish."

"Listen," Rollo said. "The law where it says bad shit drives out the good, which law is that?"

"The unwritten law," said the Greek.

The former mediator looked at him. "What are you, crazy? The unwritten law's when you catch your wife in bed with some guy."

"There's a law says some guy goes to bed with my wife?"

"No, no. The *unwritten* law."

"Well," said the Greek, "it better stay unwritten."

"That's not what I mean," said Rollo. "Hold it a second." He called to Dortmunder, "You still a double bourbon on the rocks?"

"Absolutely," said Dortmunder.

Reaching for a glass, Rollo told the nationalists, "I'm talking about the law where bad drives out good. I think it starts with G."

With obvious hesitance, the non-Turk said, "The law of gravity?"

"No, no, no," said Rollo, putting ice cubes in the glass.

"Common law," said the mediator, with absolute assurance. "That's what you're looking for."

The Greek said, "Another clown. Common law is where you aren't married to your wife, but you really are."

"That's impossible," said the mediator. "Either you're married or you're not married."

"They're both impossible," said the non-Turk.

Reaching for a bottle labeled "Amsterdam Liquor Store Bourbon—Our Own Brand," Rollo said, "That's not it. It's something else."

"Murphy's law," suggested the Greek.

Rollo hesitated, about to pour bourbon into the glass. Frowning, he said, "You sure?"

"I *think* so," said the Greek.

Neither the mediator nor the non-Turk had any comment at all. Shaking his head in continuing doubt, Rollo brought Dortmunder his drink, gesturing at the TV screen and saying, "Murphy's law."

"Sure," said Dortmunder. "The others back there?"

"The vodka-and-red-wine," Rollo said, "and a new fella to me, a rye-and-water."

That would be Ralph Winslow. Dortmunder said, "Not the beer-and-salt?"

"Not yet."

"He's late. He must have taken a wrong route."

"Maybe so," said Rollo.

Dortmunder picked up his drink and walked toward the rear of the place, past the regulars, who were now discussing Salic's law of averages. Continuing on beyond the end of the bar, Dortmunder went by the two doors marked with dog silhouettes (POINTERS and SETTERS) and past the phone booth and through the battered green door at the end into a small room with a concrete floor. The walls all around were hidden behind beer and liquor cases stacked ceiling high, leaving barely enough space in the middle for several chairs and a round wooden table covered with green felt. From a black wire over the table hung a bare bulb with a round tin reflector. Seated at the table at the moment were two people, one of them a hearty heavyset man with a wide mouth and a big round nose like the bulb of an airhorn, the other a huge mean-looking monster who seemed to have been constructed out of old truck-engine parts. The hearty man was holding a tall glass of amber liquid, clinking the ice cubes in it and looking dubiously at the monster, who brooded at a half-full glass of what appeared to be flat cherry soda. Both men raised their heads at Dortmunder's entrance, the hearty man as though in search of an ally, the monster as though wondering if this new arrival were edible.

"Dortmunder!" said the hearty man, more heartily than necessary, emphatically tinkling his ice cubes. "Haven't seen you in a coon's age!" He had a loud but gravelly voice and the permanent air of being about to slap somebody on the back.

"Hello, Ralph," Dortmunder said. Nodding at the monster, he said, "Whadaya say, Tiny?"

"I say our host is late," Tiny said. His voice was deep and not loud, like the sound emanating from a cavern in which a dragon is alleged to sleep.

"Stan'll be along," Dortmunder said. He sat with his

profile to the door, putting his glass on the felt.

"Haven't seen you since the pitcha switch," Tiny said. Incredibly, he laughed. He didn't do it well, or as though it came quite naturally, but the effort itself was praiseworthy. "I hear you had more trouble later on," he said.

"A little."

"But I got mine out of it," Tiny said. His big head nodded in slow satisfaction. "I always get mine."

"That's good," Dortmunder said.

"It's necessary." Tiny gestured with a hand like a baby bear. "I was just telling Ralph here what happened to Pete Orbin."

Ralph Winslow moodily tinkled ice. He didn't look as though he wanted to pat Tiny's back at *all*.

Dortmunder said, "Something happened to Pete Orbin?"

"I was in a little thing with him," Tiny said. "He tried to shortchange me on the cut. Said it was a mistake, he was counting on his fingers."

Dortmunder's brow corrugated. Reluctantly, he asked, "What happened?"

"I took off some of his fingers. Now he won't count on them any more." Wrapping his own sausage fingers around his glass, Tiny drained the red liquid from it, while Dortmunder and Ralph Winslow exchanged an enigmatic glance.

The door opened again and they all looked up, but it wasn't Stan Murch, who had called them all to come here tonight, it was Rollo the bartender, who said, "There's an ale outside, asking for a Ralph Winslow."

"That's me," Winslow said, getting to his feet.

Tiny pointed at his empty glass. "Again."

"Vodka and red wine," Rollo agreed. To Dortmunder he said, "It wasn't Murphy's law. It's Gresham's law."

"Oh," said Dortmunder.

"The way we found out, we called the precinct."

Rollo and Winslow left, closing the door behind them. Dortmunder worked some at his drink.

Tiny said, "I don't like this. I don't like to hang around—wait around." His heavy features were arranged in a peeved expression, like an annoyed fire hydrant.

"Stan's usually on time," Dortmunder said. He tried to stop wondering what parts Tiny removed from people who irritated him by being late.

"I got a head to break later on tonight," Tiny explained.

"Oh?"

"The cops grabbed me this morning, hung me around at the precinct two hours, asking dumb questions about that big ruby got hit."

"They're really leaning," Dortmunder agreed.

"One of them leaned too heavy," Tiny said. "Little red-headed guy. What you call your petty authority. He went too far."

"A cop, you mean."

"So he's a cop. There's still limits."

"I guess so," Dortmunder said.

"A friend of mine'll follow him home tonight," Tiny said, "to get me the address. He's on the four to twelve. Around one, I'll put on a ski mask and go to that guy's house and put his head in his holster."

"A ski mask," Dortmunder echoed. He was thinking how much good a ski mask would do to disguise this monster. In order to be effectively disguised, Tiny would have to put on, at a minimum, a three-room apartment.

The door opened again and Ralph Winslow returned, with Tiny's fresh drink and with a second man, a narrow sharp-faced type with bony shoulders and quick-moving eyes and that indefinable but unmistakable aura of a man just out of prison. "John Dortmunder," Winslow said, "Tiny Bulcher, this is Jim O'Hara."

"Whadaya say."

"Meetcha."

Winslow and O'Hara sat down. Tiny said, "Irish, huh?"

"That's right," O'Hara said.

"So's that little redheaded cop. The one I'm gonna muti-late tonight."

O'Hara looked at Tiny more alertly. "A cop? You're gonna beat on a cop?"

"He was impolite," Tiny said.

Dortmunder watched O'Hara absorbing Tiny Bulcher. Then the door opened once more, and they all looked up, and this time instead of Stan Murch it was Murch's Mom, a feisty little woman who drove a cab and was now in her working clothes: check slacks, leather jacket, and plaid cap. She looked hurried and impatient; speaking rapidly, she said, "Hello, all. Hello, John. Stan told me come by, tell you, the meeting's off."

"More impoliteness," Tiny said.

Dortmunder said, "What's up?"

"They arrested him," Murch's Mom said. "They arrested my Stan, on nothing at all."

"The police," Tiny grumbled, "are getting to become a nuisance."

"Stan says," his Mom said, "he'll call everybody again, set up another meeting. I gotta go, my cab's double-parked, there's cops all over the place."

"You can say that again," said Ralph Winslow.

However, she didn't. She merely left, moving fast.

"It's a hell of a homecoming," Jim O'Hara said. "I come back after three years upstate and there's a cop on every piece of pavement."

"It's that ruby," Tiny said.

"The Byzantine Fire," Winslow said. "Whoever grabbed that, he can retire."

"He should of retired *before*," Tiny said.

O'Hara said, "What retire? How does he convert it to cash? Nobody'll touch it."

Winslow nodded. "Yeah, you're right," he said. "I hadn't thought of it that way."

"And in the meantime," Tiny said, "he's making trouble for everybody else, forcing me to spend valuable time teaching some cop good manners. You know what I'd do if I had that guy here?"

Dortmunder drained his glass and got to his feet. "See you all," he said.

"I'd pull him *through* that ring," Tiny said. He told

Winslow and O'Hara, "You guys stick around. I don't like to drink alone."

Winslow and O'Hara watched wistfully as Dortmunder went away.

17

For Chief Inspector F. X. Mologna it had been a long long day—nearly eleven at night before he could descend to the garage beneath Police Headquarters and climb into the tan Mercedes-Benz sedan parked in the slot designated, in yellow stencil letters on the blacktop, c INSP MOLOGNA. A long day, but not an unpleasant one. He had given an exclusive interview *and* a general (and well-attended) press conference. He had thrown his weight around among a lot of federal and state officials. And he had given orders that would cause annoyance and harassment to thousands of people, one or two of whom might even turn out to have some involvement in the matter at hand. All in all, a good day.

Mologna backed out of his slot, drove up the ramp to the exit, and left Manhattan via the Brooklyn Bridge. The Brooklyn-Queens Expressway led him northeast to the Long Island Expressway, now fairly crowded with middle-class revelers returning from dinner-and-a-show in the city. As usual, Mologna listened to his police radio as he flowed eastward across Queens, hearing tonight the results of his dragnet order. One of these results was an increase in assaults on police officers, since several of the most irate arrestees had resorted to violence to express their indignation at being hauled off to the precinct for what seemed to them no good reason at all. But that too had its sunnier side; in such an incident, the cop might get a black eye, but the perpetrator would get a concussion and twenty months in Attica. Not a bad trade, from the police point of view.

Shortly after the Nassau County line, the police band faded away and Mologna switched to the regular radio, permanently tuned to an "easy listening" station—"Smoke Gets in Your Eyes," played by a million violins. Mantovani lives.

Having gone public, it would now be necessary for Mologna to keep the press informed, or at least amused, between now and the recovery of the Byzantine Fire. He was the trainer, the media people were the porpoises, and the little events—arrests, press conferences, displays of weapons caches—were the fish that made the porpoises perform. If Mologna's police blitz had not turned up the ruby by tomorrow, he'd have to throw the newsboys a few more fish. In the morning, a simple update on the number of unrelated crimes solved and criminals arrested would do, but by afternoon he'd need something more. The simplest solution—and Mologna had never seen anything wrong with simple solutions— was to release a list of eight or nine known criminals in the city whom the police hadn't as yet been able to put the arm on, announcing that these were the ones the police were most interested in questioning. The implication would be that the investigation had narrowed down to these individuals—there's progress for you—but in fact the press release would not actually *say* any such thing. Easy. Simple solutions for simple people.

Soon Mologna switched to the Southern State Parkway, where the road was free of trucks and flanked by greensward and trees. All across Nassau County the traffic gradually thinned, cars peeling off at every exit, until by the Suffolk County line—less than ten miles from home—there was a mere scattering of taillights out front and headlights in the rearview mirror. It was not quite midnight. Mologna would be in bed before one, up at nine, back behind his desk at Headquarters by ten-thirty.

Bay Shore. Mologna slowed for the exit, made the turn, and a car that had been rapidly overtaking him the last mile or so made a sharp right onto the exit as well, crowding him hard from the left.

A drunk, obviously, unfortunately not in Mologna's jurisdiction. He slowed to let the clown through.

But the clown also slowed. And there was another car also taking this exit, large in Mologna's rearview mirror. Hell of a time for a traffic jam, he thought, braked some more, and waited for the clown in the other car—green Chevrolet, absolutely unremarkable—to get under control and drive on.

But he didn't. He was angling across Mologna's lane, crowding Mologna onto the grassy shoulder, forcing Mologna to brake harder and harder—and to stop.

They all stopped. The car in front, Mologna, and the car in back. And at that point Mologna realized what was being done to him. Dry mouth, rapid heartbeat—somebody was out to get him. He reached under the dashboard for the .32 revolver he kept down there, but as he brought it out a glaring white light suddenly flooded him from the rear window of the car ahead. Blinded, blinking, he lifted the hand without the gun, shielded his eyes, turned his head away to the right, and saw movement. Outside there, having approached from the rear car, were two men, both wearing ski masks, one holding a Galil machine pistol, the other gesturing for Mologna to open the window on the passenger side.

I could pop one of them, Mologna thought. But he couldn't pop them all. And they'd made it clear—the light, the man with the machine pistol—that although they could already have popped him, they didn't intend to. At least not yet, and at least not if he didn't start popping first. So instead of popping anybody, Mologna put his revolver on the seat and pressed the button in his door that lowered the window on the other side.

The man stood well back from the car, lowering his head slightly so he could see Mologna. "Throw the gun out," he called, his voice low but carrying. He had some sort of accent; Mologna couldn't place it.

The chief inspector threw the gun out. Saliva had returned to his mouth, and his heart had slowed again. His first terror was being replaced by a lot of other feelings: anger, curiosity, irritation with himself for having been frightened.

The man stepped forward and got into the car, and as he did so the glaring light from the front car switched off, leaving the night darker than it had been. Trying to see through that darkness, Mologna studied the man beside him, who was dressed in black corduroy trousers, a dark plaid zippered jacket, and the ski mask, which was black with light-blue elks on it. He wore black-rimmed glasses over the mask, which made him look silly but no less threatening. His eyes were large, liquid, and dark. His hands were large, with short blunt fingers, chewed nails, unusually large and knobby knuckles. A workman's hands, a clerk's head, a foreign accent, and black corduroy trousers. No one in America wears black corduroy trousers.

The man said, "You are Chief Inspector Francis Mologna." He pronounced it right.

"That's fine," Mologna said. "And who would you be?"

"I have seen you on television," the man said. "You are in charge of the investigation into the disappearance of the Byzantine Fire."

"Ah-hah," said Mologna.

The man made a gesture to include the cars, his friend with the machine pistol, himself. "You can see," he said, "we are well organized and capable of swift decisive action."

"I been admirin you," Mologna told him.

"Thank you," said the man, ducking his ski-masked head in modest pleasure.

With the glaring light gone, Mologna could now see the license plate on the car in front, but there was no point memorizing it. That would be a rental car, to be abandoned half a mile from here.

"The Byzantine Fire," the man was saying, leaving off the modesty to become brisk once more, "does not belong to the government of Turkey. You will re-obtain it, but you will not give it to the government of Turkey. You will give it to us."

"And who are you?" Mologna was truly interested.

"We represent," the man said, not exactly answering the question, "the rightful owners of the Byzantine Fire. You will give it to us when it is re-obtained."

"Where?"

"We will contact you." The man looked as stern as anyone could when wearing spectacles over a ski mask. "We are, as I said, decisive," he told Mologna, "but we prefer whenever possible to avoid violence, particularly within the borders of a friendly nation."

"Makes sense," Mologna agreed.

"You drive a very nice car," the man said.

Mologna wasn't familiar with the term *non sequitur*, but he recognized the thing itself when he saw it. Still, one of the lessons life had given him was this: You go along with the man with the gun. "Sure, it is," he said.

"You have a very nice house," the man went on. "I drove past it earlier this evening. Right on the water."

"You drove past my house?" Mologna didn't like that much.

"Very expensive house, I should say." The man nodded. "I envied it, I must tell you that."

"You want a regular savins plan," Mologna told him.

"Very expensive car," the man continued, following his own obscure line of thought. "Very expensive family. Children in college. Wife with station wagon. St. Bernard dog."

"Don't forget the boat," Mologna said.

The man looked surprised, then pleased. He seemed happy for Mologna. "You have a boat? I didn't see it."

"This time of year, it's in the boathouse."

"The boathouse," echoed the man, savoring the word. "So that's what that was. Ah, to be an American. You have a boat, and you have a boathouse. How many many things you do have, after all."

"They do sort of mount up," Mologna admitted.

"How very well the Police Department must pay you," the man said.

Whoops. Mologna looked sharply through the glass in those spectacles at the eyes behind them, and those eyes seemed now to be amused, knowledgeable. So maybe the subject hadn't changed after all. "I do pretty well," Mologna said carefully.

"Astonishingly enough," the man said, "in the United States, salaries of government employees are public knowledge. I *know* what your official income is."

"You know so much about me," Mologna said. "And I know so little about you."

"For many reasons," the man said, "it seemed to us that you were the very best person to talk to in connection with the Byzantine Fire. We want it, you see. We will resort to violence if necessary, we will hunt the thief down ourselves and torture him with electric probes if necessary, but we would much prefer to be civilized."

"Civilized is nice," Mologna agreed.

"Therefore—" The man reached inside his jacket. Mologna flinched away, but what the man brought out was a white envelope. "This," the man said, hefting the envelope in the palm of his hand, "is twenty thousand dollars."

"Is it, then?"

The man opened Mologna's glove compartment and placed the envelope inside, then shut the glove compartment. "When you give us the Byzantine Fire," he said, "we shall give you another envelope, containing sixty thousand dollars."

"I call that generous," Mologna said.

"We want the Byzantine Fire," the man said. "You want eighty thousand dollars, and you do not want violence in your home city. Why should we not have a meeting of minds?"

"It don't sound bad," Mologna agreed. "But when we do get that ruby back, how'm I supposed to spirit it away? You think they'll just leave it lie around in a drawer somewhere?"

"We think, Chief Inspector, you are very imaginative, very clever, and in a position of some importance. We think you would have uses for eighty thousand dollars. We rely on your ingenuity."

"Do you, now? That's quite a compliment."

"We were very careful in choosing the right person to approach," the man said. His ski mask bunched and bubbled, suggesting that he was smiling. "I do not think," he said, "you will let us down."

"Oh, that would be cruel."

"We will contact you," the man promised. He opened the car door, stepped out, closed the door without slamming it, and went away to his own car with his armed friend. A moment later, both cars spun quickly away, and Mologna was alone.

"Well well," he said. "Well well well well well well well. Twenty thousand dollars. Sixty thousand dollars. *Eighty* thousand dollars. Great lumps of Manna out of Heaven." Taking his ring of keys out of the ignition, he locked the glove compartment, then climbed from the Mercedes, walked around it, found his revolver in the grass, and brought it back to the car. Then he drove home, where Brandy slobbered on his trousers, and he found Maureen in the family room, asleep before the TV, on which a suntanned actor chuckled meaninglessly, substituting for the substitute for Johnny Carson. Leaving Maureen where she was, absently patting Brandy, Mologna went through the house to his den, shut Brandy out, and phoned the FBI in New York. "Let me talk to Zachary," he said.

"He's home for the day."

"Put me through to him at home."

They didn't want to, but Mologna possessed a heavy, brooding, humorless authority that no minor clerk could stand up to for long, so fairly soon Zachary himself was on the line, sounding irritable: "Yes, Mologna? What is it at this hour? You found the ring?"

"A foreign fella in a ski mask offered me a bribe tonight," Mologna said. "If I would turn the ring over to him once I got it."

"A bribe?" Zachary sounded not so much astonished as bewildered, as though the very word were brand-new to him.

"Twenty thousand cash in an envelope. He put it in my glove compartment himself, with his own bare hands. I have it locked in there—I'll turn it over to the fingerprint people in the mornin."

"Twenty thousand *dollars*?"

"And sixty thousand more when I give them the ring."

"And you didn't take it?"

Mologna said not a word. He just sat there and let Zachary listen to his own monstrous question, until at last Zachary cleared his throat, mumbled something, coughed, and said, "I didn't mean that the way it sounded."

"Sure not," Mologna said. "Sorry to disturb you so late, but I wanted to report this right away. Should the good Lord in His infinite wisdom and mercy see fit to call me to His bosom this very evenin, I wouldn't want anyone to come across that envelope and think I meant to keep the dirty money."

"Oh, of course not," Zachary said. "Of course not." He still sounded more dazed than amazed.

"Good night to you, now," Mologna said. "Sleep well."

"Yes. Yes."

Mologna hung up and sat a moment in his comfortable den with the antique guns mounted on the wall, as Zachary's blurted question circled again in his mind: "And you didn't take it?" No, he didn't take it. No, he wouldn't take it. What did the man think he was? You don't get to be top cop in the great city of New York by takin bribes from *strangers*.

18

May was looking worried when Dortmunder got home, which he didn't at first notice because he was feeling irritable. "Cops stopped me twice," he said, shrugging out of his coat. "Show ID, where you going, where you been. And Stan didn't show, he was arrested. Complete mess everywhere." Then he saw her expression, through the spiraling ribbons of cigarette smoke, and said, "What's up?"

"Did you watch the news?" The question seemed heavy with unexpressed meaning.

"What news?"

"On television."

"How could I?" He was still irritable. "I been spending all my time with cops and subways."

"What was the name of that jewelry store you went to last night?"

"You can't take the watch back," he said.

"John, what was the *name*?"

Dortmunder tried to remember. "Something Greek. Something *khaki*."

"Sit down, John," she said. "I'll get you a drink."

But he didn't sit down. Her strange manner had finally broken through his annoyance, and he followed her through the apartment to the kitchen, frowning, saying, "What's going on?"

"Drink first."

Dortmunder stood in the kitchen doorway and watched her make a stiff bourbon on the rocks. He said, "You could tell me while you're doing that."

"All right. The store was Skoukakis Credit Jewelers."

"That's right." He was surprised. "That's just exactly what it was."

"And do you remember the people who came in and fussed around and then left?"

"Clear as a bell."

"They were the ones," May told him, coming over to hand him his drink, "who'd just stolen the Byzantine Fire."

Dortmunder frowned at her. "The what?"

"Don't you read the papers or *anything*?" Irritation made her puff out redoubled clouds of cigarette smoke. "That famous ruby that was stolen out at the airport," she said, "the one the fuss is all about."

"Oh, yeah, the ruby." Dortmunder still didn't make the connection. He sipped at his drink. "What about it?"

"You've got it."

Dortmunder stood there, the glass up by his mouth, and looked over it at May. He said, "Say what?"

"Those men stole the Byzantine Fire," May told him. "They put it in the safe in that jewelry store. You took it."

"I took the—*I've* got the Byzantine Fire?"

"Yes," said May.

"No," said Dortmunder. "I don't want it."

"You've got it."

Dortmunder filled his mouth with bourbon—too much bourbon, as it developed, to swallow. May pounded his back for a while, as bourbon dribbled out of his nose and eyes and ears, and then he handed her the glass, said hoarsely, "*More*," and went away to the bedroom.

When May left the kitchen with the fresh drink, Dortmunder was just leaving the bedroom with the plastic bag of loot. Silently, solemnly, they walked to the living room and sat next to one another on the sofa. May handed Dortmunder his drink, and he took a normal-sized sip. Then he emptied the plastic bag onto the coffee table, bracelets and watches all a-tumble. "I don't even know what it looks like," he said.

"I do. There was a picture on—" She picked up a ring out of the scrumble of jewelry. "That's it."

Dortmunder took it, held it between thumb and forefinger, turned it this way and that. "I remember this," he said. "I almost left it behind."

"You should have."

"At first I figured it was too big to be real. Then I figured, why put glass in the safe? So I brought it along." Dortmunder turned it over and over, peering at it, seeing the light glint and shimmer in the depths of the stone. "The Byzantine Fire," he said.

"That's right."

Dortmunder turned to her, his eyes filled with wonder. "The biggest haul of my career," he said, "and I didn't even know it."

"Congratulations." There was irony in her voice.

Dortmunder didn't notice; he was caught up in this astonishing success. Again he studied the ring. "I wonder what I could get for this," he said.

"Twenty years," May suggested. "Killed. Hunted down like a deer."

"Un," said Dortmunder. "I was forgetting."

"There's a police blitz on," May reminded him. "Also,

according to the TV, a lot of foreign guerrillas and terrorists want that ring." She pointed at it.

"And people on the street," Dortmunder said thoughtfully, "they're pretty teed off right now at whoever has this thing."

"You."

"I can't believe it." Dortmunder slipped the ring onto the third finger of his left hand, stretched the hand out at arm's length, and squinted at it. "Jeez, it's gaudy," he said.

"What are you going to do with it?"

"Do with it." That question hadn't occurred to him. He tugged the ring, to remove it from his finger. "I don't know," he said.

"You can't fence it."

"You can't fence *anything*, everybody's shook up by all this cop business." He kept tugging at the ring.

"You can't keep it, John."

"I don't want to keep it." He twisted the ring this way and that.

"What's the matter?"

"It won't—"

"You can't get it off?"

"My knuckle, it won't—"

"I'll get soap." She stood as the doorbell rang. "Maybe that's Andy Kelp," she said.

"Why would it be Andy Kelp?"

"He called, asked you to call back, said he might drop by."

"Asked me to call back, huh?" Dortmunder muttered something under his breath, and the doorbell rang again.

May went out to the vestibule to answer the door while Dortmunder, just to be on the safe side, scooped the rest of the swag back into the plastic bag. From the vestibule came May's loud voice: "Yes, officers? What can I do for you?"

Dortmunder tuuuugggggggged at the ring. No good.

"Ms. May Bellamy?"

"Maybe," said May.

Dortmunder got to his feet, opened the window, dropped

the plastic bag into the anonymous darkness.

"We're looking for a Mr. John Dortmunder."

"Oh. Well, um . . ."

Dortmunder turned the ring around so the ruby was on the inside, next to his palm. Only the gold band showed on the back of his hand.

May and two large policemen walked into the room. Looking very worried, May said, "John, these officers—"

"John Dortmunder?"

"Yes," said Dortmunder.

"Come along with us, John."

Dortmunder closed his left hand into a loose fist. The Byzantine Fire was cold against his fingers. "See you later," he told May, and kissed her on the cheek away from the cigarette, and picked up his coat, and went away with the policemen.

19

When the door to the back room at the O. J. Bar and Grill on Amsterdam Avenue opened again, about an hour after Dortmunder had left, Tiny Bulcher was just finishing a story: "—so I washed off the ax and put it back at the Girl Scout camp." Both Ralph Winslow and Jim O'Hara looked toward the door with tremulous hope in their eyes, but it was only Rollo, looking at Tiny and saying, "There's a sweet-vermouth-straight-up out here, I think he's looking for you."

"Little fella? Looks like a drowned rat?"

"That's the one."

"Kick his ass and send him in here," Tiny said. Rollo nodded and shut the door behind himself. Tiny said, "That's my pal, with that cop's address." He thudded his right fist into his left palm. "Let the good times roll," he said. Winslow and O'Hara watched his hands.

The door opened just a bit, and a narrow, pointy-nosed,

gray-skinned face peered uncertainly around the edge. The little beady eyes were blinking, and from the bloodless, down-curving mouth came a raspy whining voice: "You gonna be mad, Tiny?"

"Yes," said Tiny.

"It wasn't my fault, Tiny." The little eyes flickered at Winslow and O'Hara, found no help there, and blinked at Tiny some more. "Honest, it wasn't."

Tiny brooded at the little nervous face in the doorway. At last he said, "Benjy, you remember the time that fella told me nobody could kiss their own elbow, and then I showed him how he could?"

Winslow and O'Hara looked at one another.

"Yeah, Tiny," said the little face. Below the sharp chin a gnarled Adam's apple kept appearing and disappearing, like a pump in an oilfield.

"If I have to get up from here, Benjy," Tiny said, "and come after you, you're gonna kiss your elbow."

"Oh, you don't have to get up, Tiny," Benjy said, and he sort of spurted into the room, closing the door behind himself and revealing himself to be a skinny little stick figure of a man, all in gray, with a few strands of dead hair pasted to his narrow gray scalp. In his trembling hand he carried a glass in which the maroon vermouth made rippling wavelets. He took the chair Dortmunder had once occupied, directly across the table from Tiny.

"Comere, Benjy," Tiny said, and whumped his palm onto the chairseat beside himself.

"Okay, Tiny." Benjy sidled around the table, flashing Winslow and O'Hara quick despairing smiles, like sema-phores for help from a desert island. Slipping into the chair next to Tiny, he put his glass on the table and vermouth slopped onto the felt—not its first stain.

Tiny rested his hand on the back of Benjy's neck, in a gesture that almost looked friendly. "This is Benjy Klopzik," he told the others. "A pal of mine up till now."

"I'm still your pal, Tiny."

Tiny shook Benjy's neck gently, and the little man's head flopped from side to side. "Shut up for the introductions,

Benjy," he said, and pointed at the other two, who now were blinking almost as much as Benjy. "That's Ralph Winslow, and that's Jim O'Hara. O'Hara just got outa the can."

"How are ya?" Benjy said, with a ghastly smile.

O'Hara responded with an exercise-yard nod: small, focused, almost invisible. Winslow, in a macabre parody of his former heartiness, raised his glass, in which the tinkling ice cubes had long since melted, and said, "Nice to know you. We've all just been talking here, telling stories. Tiny's been telling us very interesting stories."

"Oh, yeah?" Benjy licked gray lips with a gray tongue. "I'd like to hear some a them, Tiny."

"I'd like to hear *your* story, Benjy." Tiny gave him another gentle shake. "You didn't get that address, did you?"

"I got arrested!"

Tiny observed the little man, who blinked back at him in desperate sincerity. Mildly, like far-off thunder, Tiny said, "Tell me about it."

"I hung around outside the precinct, just like you told me," Benjy said, "and all night the cops keep comin in with people. It's like a revolvin door. And then this cop comes over to me, and he goes, 'You look like you wanna join us. Come on in.' So they took me in and shook me down and asked me a lotta dumb questions about this big jewel—I mean," he said, appealing to Winslow and O'Hara, "do I look like a guy with a big jewel on his person?"

Winslow and O'Hara both shook their heads. Tiny shook Benjy's head. "Benjy, Benjy, Benjy," he said, more in sorrow than in anger, "I give you a simple job to do."

"Listen, I seen the guy," Benjy said. "The redheaded cop you told me about. I'll get him tomorrow, sure thing." Trying for a palsy smile, he added, "And you were sure right about him, Tiny. He kicked me in the knee."

Tiny looked interested. "Oh, yeah?"

"Then he told the other cops his tour was over, and he split. And before they let me go, he was gone."

Winslow, cranking up his heartiness, said, "Could have happened to anybody. Tough luck, Benjy."

"I'll get him tomorrow, Tiny," Benjy promised.

"It's that ruby," O'Hara said. "Nobody can do nothing. I finally hit the street and nobody can do thing one."

Tiny, almost reluctantly, released Benjy's neck—Benjy blinked like sixty in appreciation—and placed both tree-trunk forearms on the table. "That's right," he said, his voice ominous, like nearby thunder. "There's too much agitation. It's making me irritable."

Winslow said, "You'd think the law would have found the damn stone by now."

"The law," Tiny said, in disgust. "You wanna count on the law?"

"We oughta do it ourselves," Benjy piped up, then immediately looked embarrassed and terrified at having spoken. He gulped down vermouth.

They all looked at him. Tiny said, "Whadaya mean, do it ourselves?"

"Well—" Benjy, seeing retreat was impossible, rushed forward. "It's some guy in town did it, right? I mean, I know you and I know some other fellas, and you know these fellas—" with a wave at Winslow and O'Hara "—and they know some other fellas. I bet you could start here, with who else everybody knew, and draw lines, and this fella knows that fella, and by the time you're done everybody knows everybody."

"Benjy," Tiny said, leaning toward him, "if you don't say something soon that I can understand, I'm gonna whop you."

"On our side of the law!" Benjy cried desperately. "We all know each other, we all got whatchu call mutual friends. So we ask around, we look around, *we* find the ruby!"

"And the guy who copped it," O'Hara pointed out.

"Well, we take it away," Benjy said, with unconvincing bravado. "And we give the ruby to the cops, and they lay off."

"And the guy who copped it," Tiny said, "him you give to me."

"Whatever," said Benjy. "The point is, the heat's off."

Winslow said, "There's something in that idea. That's possibly a very good idea. I think I like it."

O'Hara said dubiously, "I don't know, Ralph. It kinda goes against the grain, you know? Turning somebody over to the cops."

"Somebody that made all this trouble?" Tiny flexed his fingers. "I'll turn him inside out and *then* I'll turn him over."

"Besides," Winslow said, "let's face it, Jim, people turn people over every day. That's what plea bargaining is, right? I give them you, you give them somebody else, right on down the line."

"Also," Benjy said, "there's regular stoolies. I mean, we all know guys that make a part of their living with their mouth, right? You got a mad against somebody, you go to this fella, that fella, you tell him a secret, and right away the cops know it and the guy you're mad at is on his way upstate. And the rest of the time, you watch what you tell this fella."

Tiny said, "Which fella?" He sounded as though he might be on the way to bad temper.

"The stoolie," Benjy explained, blinking. "The guy you know's a stoolie."

"Like you," Tiny told him.

"Aw, come on, Tiny," Benjy said.

"The stoolie could find out what clues the cops have," Winslow said.

Tiny brooded at him. "You mean really do it," he said.

Winslow said, "Tiny, it sounds weird, but I think we could. We got the manpower, we got the access, we got the interest."

"We'd need a center," Tiny said. "A headquarters, like. And somebody in charge."

Winslow said, "There's a phone in this room here, over there with those liquor cases. Rollo wouldn't mind. We could start calling around from here, give this number to call back for anybody has news. Different people man the phone."

"It's possible," Tiny said.

Getting to his feet, Winslow said, "I'll talk to Rollo about it." And he left the room.

O'Hara said, "I could stay here a while. Reminds me of my cell, except for no window. And it's better'n the room I got now."

Benjy was as happy as a puppy playing fetch-the-stick. Wagging his tail, he said, "It's a good idea, huh? Isn't it? Huh?"

"Benjy," Tiny said, "you go ask the cops what clues they got."

Benjy looked terribly hurt. "Aw, come on, Tiny."

"Okay," Tiny said. "Go ask a fella to go ask the cops what clues they got."

"Sure, Tiny," Benjy said. Happy again, he knocked back the last of his vermouth and bounced to his feet.

"And don't take all night."

"Sure, Tiny."

Benjy scampered from the room, and Tiny turned his heavy-browed gaze on O'Hara, saying, "What were you up for?"

"Armed robbery," O'Hara said. "My partner had a fight with his woman and she turned us in."

"A woman talked to somebody about me one time," Tiny said. "I hung her off a cornice by her pantyhose." He shook his head. "She shouldn'ta bought such cheap pantyhose," he said.

20

"And the ring," said the desk sergeant.

Dortmunder looked at his left hand. "I can't," he said. "It's stuck, I never take it off." Gazing hopelessly at the desk sergeant across the little heap of his possessions on the counter—wallet, keys, belt—he said, "It's a wedding ring."

The arresting officer on his left said, "The woman you're living with doesn't have any wedding ring."

"I'm not married to her," Dortmunder said.

The arresting officer on his right said, "What a scamp." Both arresting officers laughed.

"Okay," the desk sergeant said, and extended a form and a pen across the counter. "This is the list of your property. Read it, sign it, you'll get everything back on release."

Dortmunder had to steady the form with his left hand. The ruby tucked in among his fingers felt as big as a potato. He had to keep his hand partially closed at all times, which felt awkward and undoubtedly looked awkward. *John A. Dortmunder*, he wrote, in a rather shaky hand, and pushed the form back across the counter. His left hand eased down to his side, fingers curled.

"Come along, John," said the arresting officer on his left. He walked with them across the big room and through a door with a frosted-glass window, into a long cream corridor with pale green plastic benches lined along the left wall. At least thirty men, none of them well-dressed, sat on these benches, looking glum, or bored, or outraged, or frightened, or fatalistic, or bewildered—but never happy. Down at the far end, two blank-faced cops leaned against the wall. One of them had blue suspenders. "Sit down there, John," said one of the arresting officers, and Dortmunder took his place on the plastic bench. The arresting officers, without a farewell, departed.

Dortmunder was on line now. A door at the far end of the corridor, where the two cops leaned, would open every once in a while, and the next person on the bench would get up and go in. Nobody ever came out, though, which meant either another exit or the minotaur was inside there, eating everybody.

Dortmunder sat with his hands in his lap, fingers curled, the ruby burning a slow inexorable hole in his hand, like a laser beam. Every time the person at the end of the line went away to see the minotaur, everybody else moved leftward, wriggling their asses along the plastic benches. From time to time newer fish would arrive and be seated to Dortmunder's right. Whenever anyone spoke to his neighbor, the cops at the far end said, "Shut up, down there." The silence was heavy, muggy, discontented.

And what was the point in dragging this out? Dortmunder knew that if he simply got to his feet and showed his
left hand, palm up, the suspense would be over and done
with. All these semi-innocent people could go on home, and
Dortmunder himself could stop worrying about when the ax
would fall. Everybody would be better off—even he would.

And yet he couldn't do it. There was no hope, and yet he
hoped.

Well, no. He didn't so much hope as merely refuse to
assist Destiny in its fell designs. Every lawman in the northeast was looking for the Byzantine Fire, and Dortmunder was
seated in his local precinct *wearing* it. Disaster would arrive
when it would arrive; it wasn't up to John A. Dortmunder to
rush it along.

Three hours then passed, one moss-covered second at a
time. Dortmunder came to know that opposite wall; he was
familiar with every crack, every blemish. That particular
color of cream was permanently fixed in his brain, like a
mosaic tile. The knees of his neighbors were also well known
to him; he could probably pick them out in a lineup of hundreds of knees. Thousands.

There were a few familiar profiles to left and right along
the line, but since nobody was permitted to talk (and since
who knew what trouble you might inherit by acknowledging
in front of the cops that you did know this person or that
person), Dortmunder did no socializing. He just sat there,
and from time to time he wriggled his ass leftward on the
plastic seat, and very very slowly time passed. The cops at the
end of the hall were replaced by identical cops—neither better
nor worse—and more time grudgingly slipped through the
needle's eye of the present into the camel's stomach of the
past, until at last there was no one at all to Dortmunder's left,
which meant he was next on line. And which also meant his
left hand was extremely visible to the two cops.

Who didn't look at it. They didn't actually look at anything at all, these cops. All they did was stand there, and from
time to time murmur to one another about beer and hot dogs,
and from time to time tell somebody to shut up, and from
time to time send the next victim through the door—but they

never did look at anything, or show curiosity about anything, or give vent to a facial expression, or in any way produce at all what you could call true vital signs. They were like a memory of cops rather than the actual cops themselves.

"Next."

Dortmunder sighed. He got to his feet, left hand at his side, fingers curled, and he walked through the doorway into a pale green room lit by ceiling fluorescents, where three jaundiced men looked at him with utter cynical disbelief. "All right, John," the one behind the desk said, "come on over here and sit down."

In addition to the desk and its occupant, who was a heavyset plainclothes detective with a stubble of beard on his cheeks and some frizzy black hair around the sides of his head below the bald spot, there was on a wooden chair to the left a skinny younger plainclothes detective dressed for a picnic in jeans and Adidas and a T-shirt with a Budweiser label on it and a blue denim jacket, and on a typist's chair at the right a glum-looking, round-shouldered male stenographer in a black suit, with a little black Stenotype machine on a small wheeled metal desk in front of him. Finally in the room was a black wooden armless chair facing the desk. Like a farm horse entering its stall at the end of a long day, Dortmunder plodded to that chair and sat down.

The older detective looked very tired, but in a hostile, aggressive way, as though it were Dortmunder's fault he was so weary. He shuffled folders on his desk, then looked up. "John Archibald Dortmunder," he said. "You have been asked to come here to give the police any assistance you can in the matter of the theft of the Byzantine Fire. You volunteered to come here and talk to us."

Dortmunder frowned. "I volunteered?"

The detective looked at him as though surprised. "You weren't arrested, John," he said. "Had you been arrested, your rights would have been read to you. Had you been arrested, you would have been permitted your statutory phone call. Had you been arrested, you would have been booked and you would now have the right to have an attorney present during this conversation. You were not arrested. You were asked to cooperate, and you agreed to cooperate."

Dortmunder said, "You mean, for the last three hours out there in that hall, I've been a volunteer? All those guys out there are volunteers?"

"That's right, John."

Dortmunder considered that. He said, "What if I'd changed my mind? Out there. What if I'd decided not to volunteer after all, but just got up and left?"

"*Then* we would have arrested you, John."

"For what?"

The detective smiled a very thin smile. "We would've thought of something," he said.

"Right," said Dortmunder.

The detective looked down at the papers on his desk. "Two robbery convictions," he commented. "Two terms in prison. Lots of arrests. Recently off parole, with a positive rating from the parole officer which I personally consider a piece of shit." Looking up, he said, "You got the ruby on you, John?"

Dortmunder very nearly said yes, realizing just in time that this was cop humor, and that he wasn't supposed to respond to it at all. Cops don't like it when civilians laugh at their jokes; they only want other cops to laugh, which the one in the Budweiser T-shirt did, with a kind of half-sneeze snort, followed by, "He won't make it that easy for us. Will you, John?"

"No," Dortmunder said.

"Do you know why we picked you up, John?" the older detective asked.

"No," said Dortmunder.

"Because we're picking up known criminals," the older detective said. Then he looked across the desk at Dortmunder, obviously waiting for some sort of response.

"I'm not a known criminal," Dortmunder said.

"You're known to *us*."

It's terrible to be straight man for the cops, but they all love it so. Dortmunder sighed, then said, "I went straight, after my second fall. I got rehabilitated there in prison."

"Rehabilitated," said the detective, the way a priest might say, "Astrology."

"Yeah," said Dortmunder. "That parole report is right."

"John, John, you were picked up just last year on a TV store burglary charge."

"That was a misunderstanding," Dortmunder said. "I was found not guilty."

"According to this," the detective said, "you had some very high-powered legal help. How'd you afford that, John?"

"He didn't bill me," Dortmunder said. "I was like a charity case."

"You? Why would a hotshot lawyer come defend you for a charity case?"

"He was interested," Dortmunder said, "from a justice point of view."

The detectives looked at one another. The stenographer made delicate little finger pecks at his machine, glancing at Dortmunder from time to time in baleful disbelief and disgust. Dortmunder sat with his hands folded in his lap, his right thumb touching the Byzantine Fire. The older detective said, "Okay, John. You're an honest individual now, you only get mixed up with the law by mistake. Misunderstandings."

"It's my past," Dortmunder said. "It's hard to live down a bad past. Like you guys, right now."

"Tough," said the detective. "I feel very sorry for you."

"Me, too," said Dortmunder.

The younger detective said, "Where do you work, John?"

"I'm between jobs at the moment."

"Between jobs. What are you living on?"

"Savings."

The detectives looked at one another. Simultaneously they sighed. The older one turned his cynical eye back on Dortmunder: "Where were you last night, John?"

"Home," Dortmunder said.

"Really?" The detectives exchanged another look, and then the older one said, "Most of the boys I've talked to were playing poker last night, at each other's houses. Everybody alibis everybody else. It's like a cat's cradle." He laced his fingers, for illustration.

"I was home," Dortmunder said.

"Lots of friends and relatives there?"

"Only the woman I'm living with."

The younger detective said, "Not your wife?"

"I'm not married."

"Isn't that a wedding ring?"

Dortmunder looked down at the gold band on the third finger of his left hand. He resisted the urge to fall on the floor and froth at the mouth. "Yeah," he said. "That's what it is. I used to be married."

"A long time ago," the older detective said, tapping the folder in front of him, "according to this."

Dortmunder did not want to talk about the ring, he really and truly didn't. He didn't want people looking at the ring, thinking about it, having it in their minds. "It's stuck on my finger," he said. His heart in his mouth, he risked tugging at it a little, hoping nobody would catch a wink of ruby-red between his fingers. "That's why it didn't go with my other valuables at the desk," he explained. "It won't come off. I wear it all the time."

The younger detective chuckled. "Those old mistakes again, huh? The past just won't let go, will it, John?"

"No," Dortmunder said. He hid his left hand in his crotch.

The older detective said, "And you were not robbing any jewelry stores last night, is that right, John?"

"That's right," Dortmunder said.

The detective rubbed his eyes, and yawned, and stretched, and shook his head. "Maybe I'm getting tired," he said. "I almost feel like believing you, you know that, John?"

Some straight lines should be left alone, some rhetorical questions should be left unanswered. Dortmunder didn't say a word. He wouldn't say a word if the four of them were to sit in this room together until the end of time, until Hell froze over, until all the rivers ran dry and our love was through. He would sit here, and he would not say a word.

The detective sighed. "Surprise me, John," he said. "Give us some help. Tell us something about the Byzantine Fire."

"It's very valuable," Dortmunder said.

"Thank you, John. We appreciate that."

"You're welcome," Dortmunder said.

"Go home, John."

Dortmunder looked at him in utter astonishment. "Go home?"

The detective pointed at a door in the side wall. "Go, John," he said. "Go and sin no more."

Dortmunder got to his trembling feet, palmed the Byzantine Fire, and went home.

21

It was three-thirty in the morning, and when Rollo the bartender at the O. J. Bar and Grill got off the phone the regulars were discussing Dolly Parton. "And I say she doesn't exist," said one of them.

Another regular said, "Whadaya mean, doesn't exist? She's right there."

"All of a sudden," said the first regular. "I tell you what, you go to the library, you look in—"

"The what?"

"All right," the first regular said, "you go ahead and make jokes, but I'm tellin ya. You go look in the newspapers, the magazines, even a couple years ago, there was no such thing as a Dolly Parton. Then all of a sudden we're supposed to believe not only there *is* a Dolly Parton, there always *was* a Dolly Parton."

A third regular, bleary-eyed but interested, said, "So what's your interpretation, Mac?"

"It's that thing," the first regular said, and waved his

arms in the air. "Where everybody believes something when
it isn't so. What's that? Mass hysteria?"

"No no," said the second regular. "Mass hysteria, that's
when everybody's scared of the plague. What you're thinking
of is *folie a deux*."

"It is?"

The third regular said, "It is not. *Folie a deux* is when you
see double."

A fourth regular, asleep till now, lifted his head from the
bar to say, "Delirium tremens." Then his head lowered again.

The other regulars were still trying to decide whether or
not that had been a contribution to the discussion when a big,
gruff-looking man in a leather jacket came in and ordered a
draft. Rollo drew it, handed it over, was paid for it, and was
not at all surprised when the gruff-looking man said, "I'm
looking for a fellow called Tiny."

A lot of more or less gruff-looking men had showed up in
the last few hours, looking for Tiny or one of the others already in the back room, which must be pretty crowded by
now. "I was just going back there myself," Rollo said. "Come
along." And to the regulars he said, "It's mass delusion.
Watch the joint a minute."

The second regular said, "I thought mass delusion was
when you see the Virgin Mary in church."

The first regular said, "Where'd you expect to see her,
dummy, in a disco?"

Rollo walked down to the end of the bar, raised the flap,
stepped through, and he and the gruff-looking man walked
back past POINTERS and SETTERS and TELEPHONE. Rollo
opened the door and said, "Somebody here for Tiny."

"Whadaya say, Frank?"

"Not much," said Frank.

Rollo didn't know exactly what was going on back here,
and he didn't want to know, but he never objected to the boys
having their meetings here. And they could use the phone all
they wanted: local calls only, of course. At the moment there
were a dozen or so crowded in here, many of them smoking,
all of them drinking. The air was somewhat ripe, and a lot of

papers were scattered around on the table, and one of the
boys was making a call. That is, he was holding the phone to
his face and politely waiting for Rollo to go away.

"Listen, gents," Rollo said. "I just got a phone call I
thought I'd pass along, in case anybody's interested. It's
about that Byzantine Fire ruby."

There was a general stir in the room. Tiny growled.

"There's some foreign people the landlord knows," Rollo
said. "It was the landlord called me. These people, they're
religious or something, and they think the ruby's theirs, and
they're offering a reward. Twenty-five grand for the ruby and
another twenty-five grand if they get the guy who stole it. All
private, you know? Under the counter, no publicity."

One of the gents said, "What do they want the guy for?"

"It's some kinda religious thing," Rollo explained. "He's
desecrated the ruby, whatever. They want revenge."

Tiny said, "If *I* find the guy, I'll be happy to sell him, but
he's likely to be damaged. They'll have to take him as is."

Rollo said, "My understanding is, that's okay, just so
there's enough left so they can do their religious ceremonies
on him."

"That's one church service I'd go to," Tiny said.

"If anybody hears anything," Rollo said, "I can put you
in touch with the people offering the reward."

"Thanks, Rollo," Tiny said.

Which was a clear dismissal. Rollo went back to the bar,
where the regulars were now discussing whether jogging had
a bad effect on a person's sex life. There was also an older
man down at the other end of the bar, patiently waiting.
Rollo went behind the bar, walked down to the older man,
and said, "Haven't seen you for a while."

The older man looked surprised and pleased. "You remember me?"

"You're a whisky-and-ginger-ale."

The older man sadly shook his head. "No longer," he
said. "The doctors won't let me do anything any more. These
days I'm a club-soda-on-the-rocks."

"That's a shame."

"It certainly is."

Rollo went away and made a club soda on the rocks and brought it back. The older man gave it a look of hatred and said, "What do I owe you, Rollo?"

"When you start drinking," Rollo told him, "I'll start charging you."

"Then I'll never go broke in here." The older man lifted the glass. "To happier days, Rollo."

"Amen," said Rollo.

The older man sipped club soda, made a face, and said, "I'm looking, in fact, for a gentleman named Ralph."

Rollo was about to give him directions when he glanced toward the front windows and the sidewalk and street outside. "No, you're not," he said.

The older man looked confused. "I'm not?"

"Just sit tight," Rollo told him, as the fourteen uniformed cops swept into the place and made a beeline for the back room.

"Oh, dear," said the older man. "The doctor warned me off policemen as well."

With the fourteen uniformed cops were two plainclothes cops, one of whom came over to Rollo and said, "You're serving a lot of the wrong people here."

Rollo looked at him in mild amaze. "I am?"

"A criminal element," the plainclothesman said. "You want to watch that."

"Surprisingly enough," Rollo said, as the boys from the back room were herded past by the fourteen cops, "very few of the people who come in here tell me much about their criminal records."

"Just take it as a friendly warning," said the plainclothesman, who didn't look at all friendly.

"You guys rousted me once already!" Tiny yelled, on the way by. "I'm getting very irritated!"

"I tell you what," Rollo said to the plainclothesman. "Why don't you send me a list of the people you don't want me to serve?"

"Merely a word to the wise," the policeman said.

"Better send me two copies," Rollo told him. "I'll have to give one to the American Civil Liberties Union."

90 DONALD E. WESTLAKE

clothesman said, "it's all the same to me." Outside, there
seemed to be some difficulty convincing Tiny to join his
friends in the paddy wagon. The two plainclothesmen went
out there, withdrawing leather-covered black saps from their
rear pockets, and soon the paddy wagon and the bus and the
unmarked car all went away.

"Perhaps I shouldn't be out this late," the older man
said. He pushed his nearly full club soda away across the bar.

"Closing time," Rollo called to the regulars. They looked
thunderstruck; now they'd have to find somewhere else to go.

"It's all because of that ruby," the older man said.

"It is that," agreed Rollo.

"Whoever took it," the older man said, "I believe he'll
regret it."

"He will that," agreed Rollo.

22

Dortmunder poured beer on a bowl of Wheaties and ate, all
with his right hand, since his left rested in a pot of Palmolive
Liquid.

May said, "Are you absolutely certain I'm not asleep and
dreaming?" She sat across the kitchen table from him and
simply stared and stared.

"Maybe we both are," Dortmunder said, through a
mouthful of Wheaties and beer. He looked at his left hand.
The red ruby in the green detergent looked like a toad Cardinal in a swamp.

"Let's try it again," May said.

Dortmunder lifted his green-oozing hand out of the pot,
and while he chewed beer-soggy Wheaties, May twisted and
struggled with the ring. Simple soap hadn't done it, hot soapy
water hadn't done it—maybe Palmolive Liquid would do it.

"If I can't get that off," Dortmunder said, "I'll never be able to leave the house again. I'll be a prisoner in here."

"Don't talk about prison," May said. Shaking her head, she said, "Let it soak some more."

Dortmunder looked with loathing at the toad Cardinal in its swamp. "My greatest triumph," he said, in disgust.

"Well, in a way it is," May said. "If you stop and think about it. This has got to be just about anybody's biggest heist ever. Particularly for one man working alone."

"I can see me boasting," Dortmunder said. "To all those guys getting rousted by the law."

"Some day you'll be able to," she assured him. "This too will blow over."

Dortmunder understood that May was trying to make him feel better. What *May* didn't understand was that Dortmunder didn't *want* to feel better. Given the circumstances, any attitude in Dortmunder's mind at this moment other than frustration, helpless rage, and blank despair would be both inappropriate and a sign of mental incompetence. Dortmunder might be doomed, but he wasn't crazy.

"The day will come," May went on, "when you'll look back on all this—"

"—and get drunk," Dortmunder finished. Lifting the offending hand out of the Palmolive Liquid, he said, "Try again."

She tried again. The beveled edge of the ring grated against his knuckle. "Sorry," she said. "Maybe after—"

"Enough," Dortmunder said, put his hand in his mouth, and chomped down.

May stared, horrified. "Dortmunder!"

Palmolive Liquid tastes like used tires. Dortmunder chewed and tugged, chewed and tugged, flesh scraped raw, red blood mixed with the green detergent, and May sat there in shock, eyes as round as manhole covers. The goddamned thing fought back, but Dortmunder struggled grimly on, and at last determination won the day; removing his ringless hand from his mouth, he spat the Byzantine Fire into the pot of detergent. He would have stood up, except that May grabbed his hand in both of hers and out loud, in a shaky whispery voice, counted his fingers: "One, two, three, four, *five*. Thank God!"

Dortmunder stared at her. "Whadja think?"

"I thought— Never mind, it doesn't matter what I thought."

"Get that thing out of my sight," Dortmunder said, in re the ring, and went away to the kitchen to wash out his mouth. He was getting bubbles in his nose.

23

"Excellent prints," Zachary said, "on the envelope containing the, uh."

Mologna glinted in cold triumph across his desk at the FBI man. "Containin the *bribe*," he said. He wasn't going to let Zachary forget last night's phone call and his incredible gaffe—not for a long long time. And this was a lovely way to start a new morning: ethically and morally unimpeachable, at peace with the world, at ease in his own sunny office, toying with a couple of assholes from the FBI. "The *attempted* bribe," he went on, turning the knife.

Zachary nodded, in that manly, official, not-quite-real manner of his. "They certainly chose the wrong man, didn't they?" (Freedly gave a confirming nod.)

"They certainly did," Mologna said. "For a *bribe*. Who were they?"

"No idea, unfortunately," Zachary said.

Mologna frowned at him. "What about these excellent prints? On the envelope containin the attempted bribe?"

"Excellent prints," Zachary reconfirmed. "Unhopefully, they don't match any prints in FBI files.'

"So maybe he was a child," Mologna said. "A very tall ten-year-old, never been printed."

"We assume he was a foreign agent," Zachary said, rather stiffly. "We have turned the prints over to Interpol and to the national police forces of Turkey, Greece, Bulgaria, and Lebanon."

Mologna nodded. "A timewaster, but it'll look good on the official record." Leon pranced in, winked at Freedly, and slid a note onto Mologna's desk.

Zachary, with an annoyed little chuckle, said, "A time-waster, Chief Inspector? Do you really think these people are *also* local citizens, like your happenstantial burglar?"

"No, I don't," Mologna said, exchanging a glance with the departing Leon. "Nobody in America wears black corduroy trousers. These were some sort of Ayrabs, all right. I say what you done is a timewaster because I figure these were probably *employees* of the national police force of Turkey, Greece, Bulgaria, or Lebanon."

"Mm," said Zachary.

Surprisingly, Freedly said, "You're probably right, Chief Inspector, but it isn't a waste of time."

Mologna transferred his attention to Freedly. Having known that Zachary was an asshole, he'd naturally been assuming the assistant was another one—was that an overly hasty judgment? Yes, it was. Getting Freedly's point, Mologna nodded at him and said, "You're right."

Zachary said, "What?"

"What your partner means," Mologna told Zachary, "is now the bribers will know the bribe didn't take. Wasn't taken."

"Oh," said Zachary.

Mologna looked down at the note Leon had left: "Get rid of them," it said. Looking at Freedly again, he said, "Don't put a tail on me."

Zachary said, "What?"

Grinning at Mologna, Freedly said, "Do you want me to promise?"

"Better be ready with bail money," Mologna said.

Freedly laughed.

Zachary was becoming very red in the face. "What is all

this?" he demanded. "Just speak it out in clear and simple terminology."

Freedly explained: "Mologna sees we've set him up as a decoy."

"We have? He has?"

"And he's threatened," Freedly went on, "to have our men arrested if we put them on surveillance behind him."

"Arrested!" Zachary was shocked. "FBI men? For what?"

"Loiterin," Mologna suggested. "Public indecency. Not usin a pooper scooper. Possession for sale of a controlled substance. Traffic ticket scofflaw. Litterin the public highway."

"*Well*," Zachary said. "That isn't what *I* call interagency cooperation!"

Looking at Freedly, Mologna said, "He didn't think it through, but you did, and you should of talked it over with me first. I got children. I got a St. Bernard dog. I got a wife."

Zachary said, "What?"

Freedly said, "That's why we'll want to keep you under surveillance."

"At this stage of my life," Mologna told him, "I will not be shadowed and tailed by FBI men. You think you'll keep the newsies out? That wop Costello on the TV, he's been gunnin at me for years. Chief Inspector Mologna's under surveillance by the FBI."

"But only for your own protection," said Zachary, who'd caught up again.

"That's worse than suspicion of malfeasance in office," Mologna told him. "The top cop in the city of New York, and he has to be protected by FBI men."

Freedly said, "Sorry, Chief Inspector. You're right, of course."

"I'll watch my own back," Mologna said. "Now go away and talk to your Turks and your Greeks and your Lebanese."

"And our Armenians," added Freedly, getting to his feet.

Mologna gave Freedly a grudging nod and smile; Freedly was also an asshole, but less so than Zachary, who now also stood and said, "Chief Inspector, I assure you the FBI would never knowingly—"

"I'm convinced of that," Mologna said. "Get out of my office, I got work to do."

Zachary would have stayed, struggling for a dignified exit, but Freedly opened the door and said, "Good morning, Chief Inspector."

"Good mornin," Mologna ordered.

"We'll talk later," Zachary threatened, and at last the FBI assholes left and Leon cantered in, saying, "They *do* overstay their welcome."

Mologna brooded at him. "Who wears black corduroy pants?"

"Nobody *I* know. Captain Cappelletti's here."

Frowning, Mologna said, "That's what couldn't wait? Tony Cappelletti?"

"This time you'll like it," Leon said, and went away, returning half a minute later with Captain Anthony Cappelletti, Chief of Burglary Detail, a heavy-shouldered, big-handed, bushy-eyebrowed, bad-tempered son of a bitch with a huge blue jaw and with great spiky growths of black hair all over his person. "Good morning, Francis," he said, and pounded his feet toward the chair lately occupied by Zachary, while Leon winked over the captain's shoulder at Mologna and again exited, snicking the door shut as quiet as anything.

Early in Anthony Cappelletti's police career, it had seemed to somebody in a position of authority that he'd be an excellent man to put on the Organized Crime Detail. Not only was he Italian, he even *spoke* Italian, he'd grown up downtown in Little Italy, he'd gone to school with the sons and nephews of the *capos* and button men (who would some day be the next generation of *capos* and button men), and most important of all, Anthony Cappelletti *hated* the Mafia. *Hated* it. Just flat-out couldn't stand the whole idea of it. That of all the nationalities simmering together in this wonderful melting pot of New York City only the Italians should have their own major organized crime syndicate *with its own name* struck him as a personal affront. Was Dutch Schultz Italian? No. Was Bugsy Siegel Italian? No. Was Dion O'Bannion Italian? Hell, no! But do the Germans, the Jews, the Irish have to walk around under a cloud of suspicion, as though *all* Germans, *all* Jews, *all* Irish are mobsters? They do not! Only the Italians have to live with this general assumption that *all Italians* (with the possible exception of Mother Cabrini) *are in the Mafia.* Anthony Cappelletti found this intolerable, as though he were locked into a really bad marriage—himself and his ethnicity. It had been revulsion from the Mafia that had directed him into the police force in the first place, and the sheer obvious sincerity of his revulsion that had led the force to assign him to the Organized Crime Detail.

Where he lasted four months. "I give 'em what they understand," Cappelletti told his superiors on one of his trips to the carpet during those four months, and he sure did. He gave them so much of what they understood that in only four months he created an absolute crisis of law and order in the city of New York. Because what Cappelletti gave them, crystal-clear to their understanding, was: planted evidence, false testimony, intimidated witnesses, simple frameups, re-suborned jurors, illegal wiretaps, strongarm interrogations, and the occasional shotgun blast through a restaurant window. What he seemed to have in mind was to eliminate the Mafia completely from the Earth—that is, from New York—to do it single-handed, and to finish the job by Christmas. Within four months, though Cappelletti hadn't quite killed anybody, he'd broken so many bones, demolished so many automobiles and funeral parlors, and railroaded so many Mafiosi behind bars that the mob leaders got together at a very special private meeting in the Bahamas and there decided on the most drastic counterattack in mob history.

They threatened to leave New York.

The word got around, whispered but clear. New York might think it had lost this and that in the past—the New York Giants left for the Jersey swamps, American Airlines left for Dallas, dozens of corporate headquarters left for Connecticut, for a while even the Stock Exchange threatened to leave—but if you want *real* trouble, imagine New York if the Mafia got up and left. Think of all those mob-infiltrated businesses—with the gangsters gone, who would operate them?

The same clowns who'd run them into the ground in the first place, bailing themselves out with the black-money loans that had made the mob infiltration possible, that's who. Think of all those restaurants, linen services, finance companies, automobile dealerships, private garbage collectors, supermarkets, truck lines, and janitorial companies without the discipline, expertise, and financial depth of mob control. Think of what New York would be like with its businesses run by their nominal owners.

Beyond that, think how many policemen, politicians, newspapermen, union officials, city inspectors, attorneys, accountants, and public relations men are on the direct mob payroll. Would the City of New York like to lose that large an employer, disrupt the workforce to that great an extent?

At first the threat wasn't believed, as it hadn't been when the Stock Exchange used to talk the same way. Where would the mob move? the smart guys asked. And the answer was, anywhere they liked. The offers came in, unofficial but very tempting: Boston would be delighted to switch over from its present unreliable mix of Irish and black mobs. Miami would be overjoyed to give its Cubans the boot. Philadelphia, with nobody in charge for hundreds of years, was so desperate by now they offered to pay all moving expenses, and Baltimore was prepared to turn over four solid miles of waterfront, no questions asked. But it wasn't until Wilmington, Delaware (the "anybody-can-be-a-corporation" state), opened negotiations for the transfer of the Metropolitan Opera that New York City officials realized this was serious. "Anthony," they told Cappelletti, "you've done such a fine job on Organized Crime that we want you to take on a *really* tough assignment. Burglary Detail." Unorganized crime, in other words.

Cappelletti had known the truth, of course, but what could he do about it? He considered quitting the force, but a few tentative inquiries showed him that in all of America, only San Francisco's police department would consider hiring him, and then only to head their Flying Saucer Detail. No other police force, fire department, or any other uniformed organization in the country would touch him with fire tongs.

As for a job anywhere in mob-infiltrated private industry, that was obviously hopeless. So Cappelletti grimly accepted the change of assignment (and the sop of promotion) and took out his annoyance on every small-time, unorganized, un-influential burglar and peterman and second-story artist who came his way, with such great effect that within a couple of years he was head of the entire Detail, where he could quietly wait out his pension and brood upon injustice.

This was obviously not Chief Inspector Francis Xavier Mologna's sort of guy; they didn't hang out together much. It was, therefore, with a rather forced and false joviality that Mologna watched Cappelletti thump across his office and take a seat, glowering like a man falsely accused of being the one who farted. "So how are you, Tony?" Mologna asked.

"I could be better," Cappelletti told him. "I could use more people in Burglary."

Mologna, disappointed, said, "Is that what you're here to talk about?"

"No," Cappelletti said. "Not this time. This time I'm here on the Byzantine Fire thing."

"You found it," Mologna suggested.

"How would I do that?" Cappelletti was a very literal sort of person.

"It was a pleasantry," Mologna told him. "What have you got for me, Tony?"

"A stoolie," Cappelletti said. "He belongs to a man of mine, named Abel."

"The stoolie? Or your man?"

"My man is Abel," Cappelletti said. "The stoolie is called Klopzik. Benjamin Arthur Klopzik."

"Okay."

Cappelletti nodded his heavy head. Black hair stood in his ears, his nostrils; lines of discontent were on his cheeks. "Klopzik tells us," he said, "the street people are unhappy about the blitz."

Mologna smiled a carnivore's smile. "Good," he said.

"They're so unhappy," Cappelletti went on, "they're organizing."

Mologna's smile turned quizzical. "Revolution? From the underclass?"

"No," said Cappelletti. "They're helping us look."

Mologna didn't get it for a few seconds, and then when he did get it, he didn't want it. "The *crooks?*" he demanded. "The punks, the riffraff, they're goin to *help* us? Help *us?*"

"They want the heat off," Cappelletti said. "They figure, once we've got the ruby back, we'll ease up."

"They're right."

"I know that. They know it. So they're getting together, they're looking through their own people, they're gonna find the ruby. And the word I got, they're so teed off about this thing, they're not only gonna give us the ruby, they'll give us the guy that's got it."

Mologna stared. "Tony," he said, "I will tell you the Virgin Mary's own truth. If any other man but you came into this office and told me such a thing, I'd call him a liar and a dope addict. But I know you, Tony, I know your great flaw has always been your unimpeachable reliability, and therefore I believe you. It's a mark of the respect and admiration with which I have always beheld you, Tony. And now I want hundreds and hundreds of details."

"Klopzik came to Abel last night," Cappelletti said, "wanting to know what clues we had in the Byzantine Fire theft. Abel asked him some questions back, and they came to a meeting of the minds, and Klopzik said the headquarters of this group—"

"Headquarters! And I suppose they've got aerial reconnaissance as well."

"I wouldn't be surprised," Cappelletti said, unmoved. "It was in the back room of a bar up on Amsterdam. So we raided it and brought in eleven men, every one of them with a sheet as long as both your arms, and once our interrogators suggested cooperation might be possible, damn if all eleven didn't tell the same story as Klopzik. So we gave them our *nihil obstat* and our *imprimatur* and put them back on the street."

One nice thing about the cops—no matter how diverse

their ethnic backgrounds, they could always talk Catholic at one another. "Just so you didn't give them a plenary indulgence," Mologna said, and chuckled.

Cappelletti wasn't very lightfooted when it came to humor. Dropping the religious parallels, he said, "We got a string on them, we know where they are."

"And they're siftin the underworld, are they?"

Cappelletti nodded. "That's just what they're doing."

Mologna chuckled again. After his first indignation at the idea, he found himself increasingly amused by it. Leon had been right after all—this time he was enjoying Tony Cappelletti's presence. "Can you imagine our perpetrator," he said, "tryin out his fake alibi on *those* boyos?"

Even Cappelletti smiled at that. "I'm very hopeful, Francis," he said.

"It's lovely," agreed Mologna. "But, Tony, this has got to stay within the Department. None of our FBIers or state troopers or all them other malarkeys get to hear a word of it."

"Of course not." Since Cappelletti looked indignant all the time, it was hard for him to express it when he really was indignant.

"And bring me this Klopzik," Mologna said. "Quietly and secretly and quickly. We should get to know our new partners."

24

Dortmunder awoke to the distant sound of a ringing phone and found his left hand in his mouth. "Ptak!" he said, expelling it, then sat up, made a face around his bad-tasting mouth, and listened to the murmur of May's voice in the living room. After a minute the lady herself appeared in the doorway, saying, "Andy Kelp on the phone."

"As if I didn't have trouble enough," Dortmunder said.

But he got out of bed and plodded into the living room in his underwear and spoke into the phone: "Yeah?"

"Listen, John," Kelp said, "I got good news."

"Tell me quick."

"I'm not using the answering machine any more."

"Oh, yeah? How come?"

"Well . . ." An uncharacteristic hesitancy came into Kelp's voice. "The fact of the matter is, I was burgled."

"*You* were?"

"You remember, my message on the machine said I wasn't home. What I figure, somebody called and heard me say I wasn't home, so he came right over and boosted some things."

Dortmunder tried not to smile. "That's too bad," he said.

"Including the answering machine," Kelp said.

Dortmunder closed his eyes. He put his hand very tight over his mouth, and practically no sound at all came through.

"I could get another one," Kelp went on, "you know, from my access, like I got the first one, but I figure—"

Another voice, high-pitched and very loud, suddenly yelled, "Your father's a fairy! Your father's a fairy!"

Dortmunder jerked away from the screaming phone, no longer distracted at all by the desire to laugh. Cautiously nearing the instrument again, he heard what seemed now to be three or four shrill childish voices, giving out with some sort of nursery rhyme or something, with words that sounded like, "Hasn't got a *lump* fish. Didn't do his *dump* dish. Make her get her *plump* wish—" Through which Kelp's voice could be heard yelling, "You kids get off that phone! You get away from there or I'll come up and *getcha!*"

The nursery rhyme ended in giggles and cackles, stopping abruptly with a loud *click.* Dortmunder, enured by now, said into the phone, "You're gone, right?"

"No, no, John!" Kelp sounded out of breath. "Don't hang up, I'm still here."

"I don't really want to know what that was," Dortmunder said, "but I guess you'll tell me."

"It's my roof phone," Kelp said.

"Your *roof* phone? You live in an apartment house!"

"Yeah, well, I like to go up on the roof," Kelp said, "when the sun's shining, catch a few rays on the bod. And I don't want to—"

"Miss any calls," Dortmunder said.

"That's right. So I ran a line up, a jack, I got a phone I can bring up there and plug it in. But I guess I musta forgot to bring it back down last night."

"I guess you—"

Click: "*You've* got stinky *un*-derwear, *ding*-gles in your *pu*-bic hair—"

"Enough," said Dortmunder, and hung up and went away to the bathroom to brush the taste of his hand out of his mouth. And he was finishing breakfast half an hour later when the front doorbell rang, May answered, and Andy Kelp himself came into the kitchen, a wiry, bright-eyed, sharp-nosed fellow carrying a telephone. He seemed as cheerful as ever. "Whadaya say, John?"

"Have some coffee," Dortmunder told him. "Have a beer."

Kelp showed him the phone. "Your new kitchen phone," he said.

"No," said Dortmunder.

"Save you steps, save you time, save you energy." Kelp looked around the room. "Right there by the refrigerator," he decided.

"I don't want it, Andy."

"You'll never know how you got along without it," Kelp assured him. "I'll have it in place in fifteen minutes. You give it a trial period, a week, couple of weeks, then if you still don't like it I'll be happy—"

Kelp went on talking as Dortmunder got to his feet, walked around the kitchen table, and took the phone out of his hands. Then Kelp stopped talking and looked on open-mouthed as Dortmunder carried the phone to the kitchen window and dropped it into the airshaft.

"Hey!" said Kelp.

"I told you—" (distant crash) "—I don't want it. Have some coffee."

"Aw, John," Kelp said, coming over to look out the window. "That wasn't nice."

"You got access, right? A whole warehouse. So what I'm doing, I'm making a point. You prefer beer?"

"It's too early in the day," Kelp said, giving up on the phone. Turning away from the window, regaining his cheerful manner, he said, "I'll take the coffee."

"Fine."

Dortmunder was putting water on to boil when Kelp said, "D'jou hear the latest about that ruby?"

Dortmunder's stomach instantly became paved with concrete. Watching the pot to see if it would boil, he cleared his throat and said, "Ruby?"

"The Byzantine Fire. You know."

"Sure," Dortmunder said. He put the spoon in the instant coffee jar, but it kept hitting against the sides and knocking all the coffee off—tink-tink-tink-tink—before he could get it out. In an effort to be devious, he said, "They found it?"

"Not yet," Kelp said, "but they will. Very quick now."

"Oh, yeah?" Dortmunder emptied the instant coffee jar into the cup and spooned all but one measure back; it was the only way he could do it. "How come is that?"

"Cause we're helping," Kelp said.

Dortmunder poured boiling water on the counter, on the floor, and into the cup. "We're helping? *We're* helping? Who's 'we're'?"

"Us," Kelp explained. "Everybody. All the guys around."

Cream and sugar would be beyond Dortmunder's capacity, and even Kelp might notice something was wrong if Dortmunder poured a quart of milk on the floor. "Do your own mixings," he said, and sat down at the kitchen table in front of his own coffee cup, which he didn't feel calm enough to pick up. "What guys around?" he asked.

Kelp was rooting in the refrigerator for milk. "Tiny

Bulcher's kind of running it," he said. "Him and some other guys, using Rollo's back room at the O.J."

"At the O.J." Dortmunder felt an irrational but nevertheless poignant sense of personal betrayal. The back room at the O.J. used as the center of the hunt for *him*.

"The heat just got too much," Kelp said, coming over to the table with his coffee. He sat to Dortmunder's left. "I myself got picked up twice. Once by the transit cops!"

"Mm," said Dortmunder.

"Now, you know me, John," Kelp said. "Normally I'm an easygoing kind of guy, but when I get hauled in for no good reason twice in one day, when I got to stand around being polite to transit cops, even I say enough is enough."

"Mm mm," said Dortmunder.

"The cops have been put wise," Kelp went on. "They'll ease off, for a little while."

"The *cops*?"

"Contact was made," Kelp explained, bringing the fingertips of both hands together over his coffee cup in illustration. "A kind of arrangement was worked out. It's to everybody's benefit. The cops ease off on their blitz, we all look around, we find the guy, we turn the guy *and* the stone over to the law, everybody's happy."

Dortmunder pressed his elbows to his sides. "The guy? Turn over the guy?"

"That's the deal," Kelp said. "Besides, with what he's put everybody through, that's the least he oughta get. Tiny Bulcher wants to turn him over in sections, one piece a week."

"That seems kinda rough on the guy," Dortmunder said, as though casually. "I mean, he's just a fella like you and m-m-me, it was probably even just an accident, something like that."

"You're too good, John," Kelp told him. "In your own way, you're a kind of a saint."

Dortmunder looked modest.

"I mean," Kelp said, "even you've been rousted, am I right?"

"I spent a couple hours," Dortmunder forgivingly allowed, "at the precinct."

"We *all* did," Kelp said. "This guy, whoever he is, he's made a lot of unnecessary trouble for everybody. What he should of done was *leave the stone there*."

"Well, but—" Dortmunder stopped, trying to figure out how best to phrase what he wanted to say.

"After all," Kelp went on, "no matter how dumb he is—and this guy is dumb, John, he's grade-A dumb—no matter how dumb he is, he had to know he couldn't *sell* any Byzantine Fire."

"Maybe, uh . . ." Dortmunder had a brief coughing spell, then went on. "Maybe he didn't realize," he said.

"Didn't realize he couldn't sell the Byzantine *Fire*?"

"No, uh . . . Didn't realize that's what it was. Just took it along with, like, everything else. Found out too late."

Kelp frowned. "John," he said, "have you seen in the papers the picture of this Byzantine Fire?"

"No."

"Well, let me describe it. See, it's about—"

"I know what it looks like."

"Okay. So how dumb could—" Kelp broke off, looking at Dortmunder. "You know what it looks like? You said you didn't see it."

"I did," Dortmunder said. "I remember, I did see it. On the, on the television."

"Oh. So you know it doesn't look like something you buy the missus for Mother's Day. Anybody sees that rock, they're gonna *know*."

"Maybe," Dortmunder said, "maybe he thought it was fake."

"Then he wouldn't take it at all. No, this guy, whoever he is, he went into this thing with his eyes open, and now he's gonna get what he deserves."

"Nn," said Dortmunder.

Kelp got to his feet. "Come on along," he said.

Dortmunder's left hand clutched the chairseat. "Come along? Come along where?"

"Up to the O.J. We're all volunteering to help."

"Help? Help? What kinda help?"

"We're getting around and about, you know," Kelp said,

making swimming motions with his arms, "we're finding out where everybody was Wednesday night. We can check out alibis better than the cops, you know."

"Oh, yeah," Dortmunder said.

"Wednesday night," Kelp said thoughtfully, while Dortmunder watched him in terror. Then Kelp grinned and said, "*You* got an alibi, all right. That's the night you did your little knockover, right?"

"Ul," said Dortmunder.

"Where was that, exactly?" Kelp asked.

"Andy," Dortmunder said. "Sit down, Andy."

"Ain't you finished your coffee? We oughta go, John."

"Sit down a minute. I—I wanna tell you something."

Kelp sat down, watching Dortmunder critically. "What's wrong, John? You look all weird."

"A virus, maybe," Dortmunder said, and wiped his nose.

"Wha'd you wanna tell me?"

"Well . . ." Dortmunder licked his lips, looked at his old friend, and took his life in his hands. "The first thing," he said, "I'm sorry I dropped your phone out the window."

25

The five men seated around the kitchen table drank retsina and smoked Epoika cigarettes and spoke in guttural voices. Machine pistols hung on their chairbacks, dark shades covered the windows, and a small white plastic radio played salsa music to confound any bugging apparatus that might have been placed here by their enemies, of which there were many in this troubled old world, including the six men who abruptly crashed through the service stairwell door, brandishing their own machine pistols and in four languages ordering the men at the table not to move, nor speak, nor react in any way to their sudden appearance, lest they die like the dogs they were. The men at the table, wild-eyed and frozen, clutching their glasses and their cigarettes, muttered in three languages that the new arrivals were dogs, but made no other rejoinder.

After the first few seconds, when it became apparent that the shooting of machine pistols was not to be the first item on anybody's agenda, a cautious kind of relaxation eased all those bodies and all those faces, and everybody moved on to whatever would happen next. While two of the intruders made determined but clumsy efforts to reclose the door they'd just demolished, their leader (known as Gregor) turned to the leader of the group at the table (code name Marko) and said, "We are here to negotiate with you dogs."

Marko grimaced, scrinching up his eyes and baring his upper teeth: "What kind of debased language is that?"

"I am speaking to you in your own miserable tongue."

"Well, don't. It's painful to my ears."

"No more than to my mouth."

Marko shifted to the language he presumed to be native to the invaders: "I know where you're from."

Gregor did his own teeth-baring grimace: "What was that, the sound of venetian blinds falling off a window?"

Speaking Arabic, another of the men at the table said, "Perhaps these are dogs from a different litter."

"Don't talk like that," Marko told him. "Even *we* don't understand it."

One of the invaders repairing the door said over his shoulder, in rotten German, "There must be a language common to us all."

This seemed reasonable, to the few who understood it, and when it had been variously translated into several other tongues, it seemed reasonable to the rest as well. So the negotiation began with a wrangle over which language the negotiation would use, culminating in Gregor finally saying, in English, "Very well. We'll speak in English."

Almost everybody on both sides got upset at that. "What," cried Marko, "the language of the Imperialists? Never!" But he cried this in English.

"We all understand it," Gregor pointed out. "No matter how much we may hate it, English is the lingua franca of this world."

After a bit more wrangling, mostly for the purpose of saving face, English was at last agreed upon as the language they would use, with the solemn understanding by all parties that the choice of English should not be considered to represent any political, ethnological, ideological, or cultural point of view. "Now," Gregor said, "we negotiate."

"Negotiation," asked Marko, "comes from the barrel of a gun?"

Gregor smiled sadly. "That thing hanging on your chair," he said, "is it your walking stick?"

"Only a dog needs a gun for a crutch."

"Fine," said Gregor, switching off the radio. "Your guns and our guns cancel each other. We can talk."

"Leave the radio on," Marko said. "It's our defense against bugging."

"It doesn't work," Gregor told him. "We've been bugging you from next door, with a microphone in that toaster. Also, I hate salsa music."

"Oh, very well," Marko said, with bad grace. (The radio as a defense against bugging had been his idea.) To his compatriot opposite him across the table, he said, "Get up, Niklos, let this dog sit down."

"Give my seat to a dog?" cried Niklos.

"When you negotiate with a dog," Marko pointed out, "you permit the dog to sit."

"Be careful, Gregor," one of the invaders said. "Watch where you sit, that dog may leave you fleas."

The two repairman-invaders at last wedged the door shut and came over to the table. One of them said, "Did you ever notice how you don't get the same *effect* when you call somebody a dog in English?"

One of the men at the table said, "The Northern peoples are cold. They put no fire in their tongues."

Seating himself in Niklos' place at the table—Niklos sullenly leaned against the refrigerator amid his enemies, arms folded—Gregor said, "We have been enemies in the past."

"Natural enemies," the other said.

"Agreed. And we shall be enemies again in the future."

"God willing."

"But at this moment, our requirements intersect."

"Meaning?"

"We want the same thing."

"The Byzantine Fire!"

"No. We want," Gregor corrected, "to *find* the Byzantine Fire."

"It's all the same."

"No, it's not. When we know where it is, we can contest properly for its possession. At that time, our desires shall again be in opposition, and we shall again be enemies."

"From your lips to God's ear."

"But so long as the Byzantine Fire is lost, we find ourselves, however uneasily, *on the same side.*"

There was general bristling at such an idea, until Marko raised his arms in a commanding gesture, as though calming a multitude from a balcony. "There is sense in what you say," he admitted.

"Of course there is."

"We are all aliens in this godless land, however many contacts we may have among the émigrés."

"Emigrés," spat Gregor. "Petty merchants, buying aboveground swimming pools on the installment plan."

"Exactly. You can force a man to fetch and carry and obey orders if you threaten him with the death of his grandmother in the old country, but you can't get him to *think*, to *volunteer*, to show you the inner workings of this debased and sensualist society."

"Our experience precisely."

"Strangers in a strange land would do well to combine their forces," Marko mused.

"Which is just what I'm here to recommend. Now, we have made an initial exploratory contact with the police." (Gregor wore black corduroy trousers.) "And you have made initial exploratory contact with the New York underworld."

Marko (it was his uncle who knew the landlord at the O.J.) looked surprised at that, and not at all pleased. "How do you know such a thing?"

"Your toaster told us. The point is, we can complement one another's scanty intelligence, and we can be prepared to act decisively when the Byzantine Fire is found, and—"

"Also the thief," Marko said.

"We have no interest in the thief."

"We do. For religious reasons."

Gregor shrugged. "Then we'll turn him over to you. The main point is that, combining together, the chances of our finding the Byzantine Fire are much improved. Once it's found, of course, we can discuss the next step. Are you agreed?"

Marko frowned around at his men. They looked tense and bony-cheeked and grim, but not violently opposed to the suggestion. He nodded. "Agreed," he said, and extended his hand.

"May the souls of my ancestors understand and forgive this expediency," said Gregor, and grasped his enemy's hand.

The phone rang.

The men all stared at one another. The leaders wrenched their hands apart. Gregor hissed, "Who knows you're here?"

"No one. What about you?"

"No one."

Getting to his feet, Marko said, "I'll deal with it." He crossed to the wall phone, unhooked the receiver, and said, "Allo?" The others watched him, saw his expression darken like the sky before a summer storm, saw it then redden (sailors take warning), saw it then look merely confused. "One moment," he told the phone, and turned to the others. "It's the Bulgarians," he said. "They've been bugging us from the basement, they heard everything, they say it makes perfect sense. They want to come up and join us."

26

"Gee muh *knee*," Kelp said, gazing at the Byzantine Fire.

"Don't put it on," Dortmunder advised him. "I had a hell of a time getting it off."

"Jeez," Kelp said. He just sat there in the living room, on Dortmunder's sofa, staring at the ruby and the sapphires and the gold all glittering away in his palm. "Holy shit," he said.

May, hovering like a den mother, said, "Would you like a beer, Andy?"

Dortmunder told her, "It's too early in the day for him."

"The hell it is," said Kelp.

"Better make it two, then," Dortmunder said.

"Three," said May, and went off to get the beers, trailing cigarette smoke.

Dortmunder went and sat down in his favorite easy chair, facing the sofa. He watched Kelp watching the Byzantine Fire until May came back, when Kelp's attention was finally distracted by a can of beer. Then Dortmunder said, "So that's it."

Kelp looked at him over the beer can. "Jeez, John," he said. "How'd it happen?"

So Dortmunder told him how it had happened; the breaking in, the guys arriving, the guys leaving, the finding of the stone. "Who knew what it was?" Dortmunder finished.

"Who knew what it was?" Kelp echoed, incredulous. "The Byzantine *Fire*? *Everybody* knows what it is!"

"They do now," Dortmunder pointed out. "Wednesday night, it had just been robbed, it wasn't all over the papers yet, *nobody* knew any Byzantine Fire."

"Sure they did. It was too in the papers, the American people were giving it to Turkey, that's how come it came in from Chicago."

Dortmunder gave Kelp his steadiest look. "Andy," he said, "that's something else you know *now*, it's part of the robbery story. Tell me the truth: before the heist, did you know all about this American people gift business?"

Looking a bit uncomfortable, Kelp said, "Well, in a general sort of way."

"It could of happened to you," Dortmunder told him. "Don't kid yourself. You could of been the one noticed the vacation sign, broke in, opened the safe, saw that big red rock and figured, what the hell, take it along, maybe it's worth something. It could of happened to you."

"It didn't, John," Kelp said. "That's all I can say, and I'm happy I can say it. It *didn't* happen to me."

"It happened to me," Dortmunder said, and was grimly aware that all three people in the room—including, God help him, himself—were thinking about the Dortmunder jinx.

Kelp shook his head. "Wow," he said. "Whadaya gonna do now, John?"

"I don't know. I didn't realize I even had the goddam thing till last night, I haven't had much time to think about it."

"I hate to say this to any man," Kelp said, "but I think you oughta give it back."

Dortmunder nodded. "I been thinking the same way. But it raises a question."

"Yeah?"

"How? How do I give it back? Do I mail it?"

"Don't be silly, you know you can't trust the mails."

"Also," Dortmunder said, "I don't feature just leaving it someplace, like one of your abandoned babies in church, because then some kid comes along or some wise guy, and he grabs it, and the heat stays on, and I'm *still* in trouble."

"You know what, John?" Kelp sat up straighter on the sofa. "A sudden thought just hit me."

"Yeah? What's that?"

"You better not go to the O.J., after all. I don't think you could safely chit-chat with Tiny Bulcher. I mean, face it, you don't have an alibi."

Dortmunder said nothing. He just looked at Kelp. It was May, seated in her own chair to one side, who said quietly, "John knows that, Andy."

"Oh, yeah? Yeah, I see what you mean." Kelp grinned

and shook his head at himself, saying, "This is still new news to me, you know? I'm still catching up."

"The thing right now," Dortmunder said, "is how do I give that goddam ruby back."

"I think you gotta call them," Kelp said.

"Who, Turkey? Or the American people."

"The law. Call that cop on the television, Maloney." (Having only heard the name and never having seen it, that's the way Kelp thought it was spelled.)

"Call the cops," mused Dortmunder. "And then I say, 'Hello, I got it. You want it back?' "

"That's right," Kelp said. He was getting excited. "Then you maybe even dicker a little. John, you could maybe even turn a profit on this thing!"

"I don't want to turn a profit," Dortmunder told him. "I just want out from under that stone."

"Well, keep an open mind," Kelp suggested. "See how the conversation goes."

"I'll tell you how the conversation goes," Dortmunder said. "We dicker back and forth, we keep an open mind, and meantime they're tracing the call, and all of a sudden I'm surrounded by blue uniforms."

"Not necessarily," Kelp said, looking very thoughtful.

May said, "Andy? Do you have an idea?"

"Could be," Kelp said. "*Coouuuuld* very well be."

27

When the little man sidled into the office, ushered by Tony Cappelletti, Mologna gazed sternly across his desk and said, "Benjamin Arthur Klopzik?"

"Gee!" the little man said, with a sudden huge beaming smile. "Is that *me*?"

Mologna frowned and tried again: "You are Benjamin Arthur Klopzik?"

"I am?"

"Siddown," Tony Cappelletti told the little man, giving him a shove toward the chair in front of Mologna's desk. "This is Klopzik, all right. You trying to pull something, Benjy?"

"Oh, no, sir, Captain," Benjamin Arthur Klopzik said, and turned an appealing little smile in the direction of Mologna. "Good morning, Chief Inspector."

"Go to hell," Mologna told him.

"Yes, sir." Klopzik placed his dirty-nailed hands between his bony knees and sat very alertly, like a dog who can do tricks.

"So," Mologna said, "a lot of you social misfits, penny-ante heisters, cheapjack four-flushers, and miserable hopeless losers figure you'll help the Police Department of the City of New York find the Byzantine Fire, is that it?"

"Yes, sir, Chief Inspector."

"Not to mention the FBI."

Klopzik looked confused. "Chief Inspector?"

"Not that I *want* to mention the FBI," Mologna went on, and looked past Klopzik to toss a wintry smile at the still-standing Tony Cappelletti, who gave nothing back at all; it was like telling a joke to a horse. Mologna wished Leon wouldn't spend so much time in the outer office, doing his crochet. Was there an excuse to buzz for Leon? Frowning severely at Klopzik, Mologna said, "So you'll make a statement, is that right? And sign it?"

But Klopzik looked terrified: "Statement? Sign?" Twisting around in his chair, he stared mutely at Cappelletti, as though at his trainer.

Who shook his heavy hairy head. "We don't want to blow Benjy in the underworld, Francis."

No statement, then, and therefore no Leon. "All right," Mologna said. "Klopzik, there's no deal involved in this, you understand that. If you bums and parasites and miserable scum decide to help the authorities in their investigations into this heinous crime, it's strictly public spiritedness on your side, you got that?"

"Oh, sure, Chief Inspector," Klopzik said, happy again. "And in the meantime, the blitz is off, isn't that right?"

This time, the full frigid force of Mologna's wintry smile was directed at Klopzik, who blinked under it as though he'd developed immediate frostbite of the nose. "You call that a blitz, Klopzik?" Mologna demanded. "You think that little exercise we've had up till now deserves the word *blitz*?"

Mologna stopped there, waiting for an answer, but he might as well have saved saving his breath. The mind of Benjamin Arthur Klopzik was nowhere near intricate enough to figure out whether the right answer was *yes* or *no*. Mologna waited, and Klopzik sat blinking at him, alert for an order to roll over or fetch a stick, and at last Mologna answered the question himself: "It does not," he said. "*Tomorrow*, if we're still lookin for that blessed ruby, you and all your riffraff ne'er-do-well friends will have a golden opportunity to see what a real blitz looks like. Do you want that, Klopzik?"

Klopzik knew *that* answer: "No, Chief Inspector!"

"You go back and tell that gang of ruffians what I said."

"Yes, Chief Inspector."

"And you can also tell those hooligans and boyos, as far as I'm concerned they aren't doin me or the Police Department or the City of New York any favors."

"Oh, no, Chief Inspector."

"Their civic duty is all they're performin, and the sweet Virgin knows it's overdue."

"Yes, Chief Inspector."

"They'll get no thanks if they succeed, and they'll feel the wrath of my fist if they fail."

"Yes, Chief Inspector. Thank you, Chief Inspector."

"And when I say—"

The door opened and Leon drifted in, like Venus toward shore. "You'll never believe this one," he announced, while Tony Cappelletti surveyed him with the gloomy frustration of a muzzled St. Bernard studying a cat.

"Hold it, Leon," Mologna said, and went on with his sentence: "When I say *tomorrow*, Klopzik, do you know what I mean?"

Wrinkles of bewilderment further marred the little man's features. "Yes, Chief Inspector?"

"I'll tell you what I mean," Mologna warned him. "I do *not* mean whenever it is you drag your miserable carcass out of your vermin-infested bed."

"No, Chief Inspector."

"I mean *one second* after midnight, Klopzik. *That's* tomorrow."

Klopzik nodded, extremely alert and receptive. "Midnight," he echoed.

"Plus one second."

"Oh, yes, Chief Inspector. I'll tell Tuh—my friends. I'll tell them just what you said."

"You do that." To Cappelletti, Mologna said, "Take it away, Tony, before I forget myself and polish my shoes with it."

"Right, Francis." Cappelletti cuffed Klopzik almost amiably across the top of the head. "Come along, Benjy."

"Yes, sir, Captain," Klopzik said, spurting to his feet. "Good morning, Chief Inspector."

"Go fuck yourself."

"Yes, sir!" Klopzik turned his happy face toward Leon: "Good mor, morn, uh . . ."

"Out, Benjy," Cappelletti said.

"You're cute," Leon told Klopzik, who left the room looking suddenly glazed and uncertain.

When they were alone, Mologna said, "Leon, don't you overstep the bounds of good taste."

"Oh, I couldn't."

"That's good. Now, tell me what it is I won't believe."

"The thief just called," Leon said, with the kind of little smirk that means there's more than that to the story.

"The thief. The *thief*?"

"The man with the ruby in his bellybutton," Leon agreed. "The very one."

"But that's not the part I'll not believe."

"Oh, no," Leon said, and actually giggled. "See, he called asking for you—he got the pronunciation right and everything—so they put him through to me."

"How'd he sound?"

"Nervous."

"He damn well oughta be. So what happened?"

"I said you were in conference and could you call him back at ten-thirty, and he said yes."

Leon stopped there, swaying, dancing in place to some inner rhythm, grinning with barely repressed mirth. Mologna frowned at him, feeling stupid, not getting it. "So? What happened next?"

"Nothing," Leon said. "He hung up. But don't you *see*? I said you'd call him back. *He gave me his phone number!*"

28

When Dortmunder got off the phone with Chief Inspector Maloney's (he also thought it was spelled that way) secretary—an odd-sounding guy for a cop—he was so drenched in perspiration that he took a shower in Andy Kelp's bathroom, emerging clad in Andy's robe (too short) to find a note on the kitchen table: "Out for lunch. Back in 10 min." So he sat with the *Daily News* and read about the manhunt for himself until Kelp came back with Kentucky Fried Chicken and a six-pack. "You're looking more relaxed already," Kelp said.

"I am not," Dortmunder told him. "I look like somebody with a disease. I look like somebody's been in a dungeon for a hundred years. I've seen myself in your mirror, and I know what I look like, which is exactly what I am: a man that made Tiny Bulcher mad."

"Look on the bright side," Kelp advised, distributing beer and chicken legs here and there on the kitchen table. "We're fighting back. We're working on a plan."

"If that's the bright side," Dortmunder said, cutting his thumb as he opened a beer can, "there's no point looking at it."

"While I was out," Kelp said, touching all the chicken

legs in the bucket before making his choice, "I set things up for the phone call."

"I don't even like to think about it."

Kelp ate chicken. "It's a piece of cake."

Dortmunder frowned at the kitchen clock. "Half an hour." He picked up a chicken leg, studied it, put it down again. "I can't eat." Standing, he said, "I'll go get dressed."

"Drink your beer," Kelp suggested. "It's got food value."

So Dortmunder took his beer away and got dressed, and when he came back Kelp had eaten all the chicken legs but one. "I saved that for you," he said, pointing at the thing, "in case you changed your mind."

"Thanks a lot." Dortmunder opened another beer without cutting himself and gnawed a bit on the chicken leg.

Getting to his feet, Kelp said, "Lemme show you my access. Bring the leg."

Kelp's bedroom was behind the kitchen. Carrying the chicken leg and the new beer, Dortmunder followed him back there and into the closet, which turned out to have a false rear wall made of a single piece of Sheetrock. Removing this, revealing a brick wall with an irregular opening about five feet high and a foot and a half wide, Kelp grasped two suction-cup handles attached to a piece of wallboard beyond the bricks and did a complicated little lift-tug-twist-*push* which made that wallboard recede, exposing a dim, crowded-looking space beyond.

Kelp took a step through the hole into this space, still grasping the wallboard by the suction-cup handles, and twisted his body sidewise to get through the narrow opening in the bricks. Dortmunder watched him, dubious, but when Kelp was all the way through with no alarms or shouts or other hooraw, Dortmunder followed, slithering through into an obvious warehouse, lined with rows of rough-plank shelves and bins, all piled high with large or small cardboard cartons. Gray light hovered in the air from distant grimy windows.

Kelp, sliding the wallboard segment back into its slot, whispered, "We got to be quiet now. There's workers down at the front of the building."

"You mean *now*? There's people in here *now*?"

"Well, sure," Kelp said. "It's Friday, right? A working day. C'mon."

Kelp led the way down the nearest aisle, Dortmunder tiptoeing after. Kelp moved with absolute assurance even when the echoing sound of semidistant voices was heard, and eventually Dortmunder followed him through a windowed door into a smallish room where telephones and telephone equipment were displayed on tiny walnutish shelves on orange pegboard fronting all four walls. "Here we go," Kelp said, the compleat salesman. "Phones here, add-ons there, recording and playback equipment over there."

"Andy," Dortmunder said, "let's do it and get it over with."

"Well, make your selection," Kelp told him. "Whadaya want? Here we got a nice pink Princess, light in the dial, remember the Princess?"

"I remember the Princess," Dortmunder agreed. "You couldn't dial it, and you couldn't hang it up."

"Not one of our best designs," Kelp admitted. "Now, over here we got something Swedish. I notice this particular model is avocado, but you're not limited in color, we got every color you want. Here, give this a heft."

Dortmunder, having put down his beer can with the chicken leg balanced atop it, found himself holding the avocado something Swedish. It looked like minimalist modern sculpture, shaped somewhat like a horse's neck, curving and narrowing up from a not-quite-round base, then arcing at the top into what was apparently the part you listened to. And the little black holes down near the base were probably where you talked. Turning this object upside down, Dortmunder saw the dial on the bottom, surrounding a large red button. He pushed the button, then released it.

"Very popular," Kelp said, "with the trendy set. One little warning, though—if you put it down to like get a pencil, light a cigarette, you break the connection."

"Break the connection? I don't follow."

"It's like hanging up," Kelp explained. "That red button on the bottom hangs it up."

"So if I'm talking on this thing," Dortmunder said, "I

can't put it down because then I'll hang up."

"You have to put it down on its side."

Dortmunder put the thing down on its side. It rolled off the shelf and fell on the floor.

"Then," Kelp said, turning away from the Swedish something, "we've got this little number from England. Very lightweight, very advanced design."

Dortmunder frowned at this new option, sitting like a praying mantis on its shelf. It was shaped more or less like a real phone, but it was smaller and colored *two* shades of avocado and made from the same kind of plastic as model Stukas and Stutzes. Also, it didn't have any rounded surfaces, just flat surfaces that met at funny angles. Dortmunder picked up the receiver and closed his hand around it and the receiver disappeared; a little bit of plastic stuck out of Dortmunder's mitt at each end, like segments of a mouse on both sides of a cat's smile. He opened his hand and looked at how close the ear-part and the mouth-part were, then held it tentatively to his cheek, then frowned at Kelp and said, "This is for people with tiny heads."

"You get used to it," Kelp assured him. "I've got one of those in the hall closet."

"In case you're hanging up your coat when the phone rings."

"Sure."

Dortmunder poked the other part of this English number with his finger, planning to dial it, but the phone jittered away as though ticklish. He pursued it as far as the wall, where he got halfway through dialing a "6" when the phone loused him up by turning with him. "You need two hands to dial it," he objected. "Just like the Princess."

"It is better," Kelp conceded, "on incoming calls."

"From the Munchkins. Andy, all I want's a phone."

"How about this one shaped like Mickey Mouse?"

"A phone," Dortmunder said.

"We haven't even talked push buttons."

"Andy," Dortmunder said, "do you know what a phone looks like?"

"Sure. But take a look at this one in its own briefcase,

built right in. Carry it anywhere, plug it in. Here's one with a blackboard on it, you can take messages, write them down with chalk."

While Kelp continued to point this way and that, calling Dortmunder's attention to things of no interest, Dortmunder picked up his chicken leg and beer, chewed and drank, and scanned the orange wall, searching, searching . . . until finally, on the lowest shelf way over to the right, he saw a phone. A real phone. Black, with a dial. Shaped like a phone. "That," Dortmunder said.

Kelp paused in his contemplation of a seven-eighths-size modern facsimile of an old wall-type crank phone. Looking at Dortmunder, he said, "What?"

"That." Dortmunder pointed the chicken leg at the real phone.

"That? John, whadaya want with *that*?"

"I'll talk on it."

"John," Kelp said, "even bookmakers wouldn't use a phone like that."

"That's the one I want," Dortmunder said.

Kelp considered him, then sighed. "You sure can get stubborn sometimes," he said. "But, if that's what you want . . ."

"It is."

Gazing sadly at all those rejected wonders, Kelp shrugged and said, "Okay, then, that's what you'll get. The customer is always right."

29

"It's a pay phone," Tony Cappelletti said, "in the Village, on Abingdon Square."

"My men," Malcolm Zachary said firmly, like an FBI man, "can have that booth staked out in five minutes."

Mologna glowered heavily across his desk. Cooperation

between law enforcement agencies had made it necessary to bring the FBI in on this phone call from the alleged thief, but it wasn't necessary to put up with a lot of disguised feds saturating the area in laundry trucks and unmarked black sedans with D.C. plates. "So far," Mologna said, "this is a crank call to the Police Department of the City of New York. We're not goin to make a federal case out of it."

"But," Zachary said, "we have infiltratory specialists, men carefully trained to blend into any environmentalism."

"The New York Police Department," Mologna said, "has men who can blend into the environmentalism of New York City."

"Equipment," Zachary said, beginning to look desperate. "We have walkie-talkies that look like ice cream cones."

"That's why *we'll* handle the case," Mologna told him. "Our walkie-talkies look like beer cans in brown paper bags." Having finished off Zachary, Mologna turned back to Tony Cappelletti: "Our people in position?"

"All ready," Cappelletti promised. "We've set up our war room across the hall."

Mologna crouched over his massive belly like a man catching a beach ball, then all at once heaved himself to his feet. "Let's go," he said, and marched out, trailed by the dour Cappelletti, the sparkling-eyed Leon, the disgruntled Zachary, and the watchful-but-silent Freedly.

In a bare room across the hall, some long folding tables and rickety folding chairs had been set up on the scuffed linoleum floor, a few phone lines and radio equipment had been brought in (their cables flopped around underfoot), a couple of city and subway maps had been taped to the wall, and two overweight black women and an overweight white man in grungy civilian clothing sat around smoking cigarettes and discussing retirement benefits. As a war room, it would have made James Bond laugh.

The newcomers clustered around a city map on one wall, and Tony Cappelletti described the current situation: "Abingdon Square is here in the West Village, at the meeting of Bleecker, Hudson, Bank, and Bethune streets and Eighth Avenue. Hudson and Bank are the only through streets, so we've got a total of seven entrances or exits to the square. The phone we're after—"

"The target phone," murmured Zachary.

"—is here at the corner of Bleecker and Bank, south side, directly in front of the children's playground. It's a very open area, because of the playground on the south and very wide Eighth Avenue to the north."

"What's our stakeout?" Mologna asked.

"In the playground itself," Cappelletti said, "we got two vendors, one selling hot dogs, the other selling cocaine. In a restaurant on Bleecker across the street from the phone we got a TPF squad, fully equipped, and—"

Freedly, the less assholish FBI man, broke his long silence to say, "Excuse me. TPF?"

"Tactical Patrol Force," Mologna told him. "Those are our head-beaters."

Freedly frowned. "Crowd control, you mean?"

Zachary echoed, "Crowd control? Inspector, we aren't dealing here with dissentation, some sort of anti-this, anti-that demonstration. This is a robber, in a negotiatory posture."

Mologna sighed, shook his head, and resigned himself to patience. "Zachary," he said, "do you know what the West Village is?"

"A part of Greenwich Village," Zachary said, frowning sternly. "Of course I know where it is."

"Not where. *What.*" Holding up three fingers, Mologna said, "The West Village is three separate and distinct small-town communities all existin in the same space at the same time. They are first the ethnic community, which is mostly Italian plus Irish, and which used to be two communities that knifed each other a lot but now they've got together against numbers two and three. Two is the artsy-craftsy community, everythin from folk singers and rug hookers and candle dippers to hotshot TV personalities and writers with their own column in the papers. And three is the fag community, which makes *Alice in Wonderland* look like a documentary. Any time

we make an arrest in that area, we run the risk of offendin one
or more of those communities, and if we *do* offend one or more
of those communities the TPF comes out and breaks heads
until we can retreat back to the United States. You follow me
so far?"

While Zachary merely blinked and nodded, looking
forceful though bewildered, Freedly said, "The map is not the
terrain."

Mologna nodded at him. "You're right."

"Von Clausewitz said that," Freedly added.

"He knew his onions." Mologna turned back to Cappelletti: "What else we got?"

"A city bus broken down here on Eighth Avenue," Cappelletti said. "That gives us a driver and two mechanics. Two
winos here on Hudson Street, lying in a doorway. Sanitation
Department truck here on Bethune, four men, goofing off.
Pair of chess players here, at the benches just south of the
playground. Little old lady with a lot of shopping bags handing out Jesus Saves pamphlets here at the corner of Bank and
Hudson."

"Hold on," Zachary said, hitching up his trousers like an
FBI man. "What is all this? Sanitationmen, little old ladies.
Who is this little old lady?"

"He's a police officer," Tony Cappelletti said, while Mologna and Leon exchanged a glance. "He's usually a decoy
with the mugging detail. I've seen him, Francis," he added to
Mologna, "and he does an old lady so good you wanna ask
him to make you an apple pie."

Zachary said, "The bus driver, the garbagemen—"

"Sanitationmen," Mologna said.

"They're all police officers?"

Even Tony Cappelletti was prepared to exchange a
glance with somebody at that one; he exchanged it with
Freedly, who said, "If *we* were doing it, Mac, our people
would also be in disguise."

"Well, of course they would! The description was just a
little confusing, that's all." Frowning manfully at the map,
Zachary said, "You appear to have the target phone well
encircled."

"You bet your ass we do," Mologna told him.

"That's fourteen men," Cappelletti said, "with visual contact on the phone. Plus the TPF in that restaurant, plus two more squads out of sight some distance away—here in a parking garage on Charles Street, and over here in a moving company garage on Washington Street."

Leon said, "Ding dong."

Everybody turned to look at him. Mologna, not quite believing it, said, "Leon? Was that you?"

Leon mutely pointed at the big white clock on the wall, and when everybody turned that way they saw the time was precisely ten-thirty. "Okay," Mologna said. "Unconventional, Leon, but okay."

Leon smiled. "I can do a perfect Big Ben, quarter hours and everything."

"Later." Looking around, Mologna said, "Which phone do I use?"

"This one, Francis." Cappelletti ushered Mologna to a phone on one of the long tables. Seating himself on a folding chair—it shrieked in agony—Mologna reached for the receiver, poised his finger over the push buttons, then stopped and frowned. "What's the number?"

Everybody patted his pockets and it turned out Cappelletti had it, on a crumpled piece of paper, which he smoothed out and placed on the table. Mologna dialed, while one of the black women who'd been sitting around talking about retirement benefits spoke quietly into a microphone, saying, "He's making the call now."

Three miles away, at Abingdon Square, two winos, four sanitationmen, a bus driver, two vendors, two mechanics, a pair of chess players, and a little old lady all tensed, watching and waiting, their attention on a shiny, small telephone-on-a-stalk. Not even an enclosed booth; just a small three-sided box on one leg.

"It's ringin," Mologna said.

"It isn't ringing," the black woman at the microphone said.

Mologna frowned at her. "No no, I said it *is* ringin."

She shrugged. "The folks on the street say it isn't ringing."

"What?" Mologna said, and a voice in his ear said, "Hello?"

"Phone ain't ringing," the black woman said. "Maybe it's busted."

"But," Mologna said, and the voice in his ear said, "Hello? Hello?" So he said it right back: "Hello!"

"Oh, there you are," the voice said, sounding relieved.

Mologna said, "And who the fuck are you?"

"I'm the, uh . . ." He sounded rather nervous and had to stop to clear his throat. "I'm the guy, you know, the guy . . . with the, uh, I'm the guy with the thing."

"The thing?" Bewildered faces were crowding around Mologna now.

"Ring. The ring."

Zachary said, "Who in God's name are you talking to?"

Waving Zachary and everybody else away, Mologna said, "*Where* are you?"

"Well, uh . . . I don't think I oughta tell you that."

The black woman was speaking with muted hysteria into her microphone. Three miles away, the pay phone in question sparkled in morning sunlight, alone, unringing, unoccupied, innocent and virginal. A cocaine salesman drifted slowly by it and repeated the phone's number aloud to his beer can. Two winos staggered to their feet and stumbled across the square toward the children's playground. The sanitationmen started their truck engine.

Mologna said, "God damn you, son of a bitch, what's goin on here?"

"It's the right number," the black woman said.

The other black woman, who'd been talking quietly but hurriedly into another phone, now said, "The phone company says the call's going through."

"See," the voice in Mologna's ear said, "I just want to give it back, you see what I mean?"

"Hold on," Mologna told the phone, cupped the mouthpiece, and glared at the second black woman. "What was that you said?"

"The phone company says the call's going through. They say you're talking to somebody at that pay phone."

Three miles away the chess players folded up their unfinished game, while their kibitzers said things like, "Are you crazy? Man, what's the matter with you? Man, you was three fuckin moves from mate, man." The pamphlet-distributing little old lady had crossed Hudson Street and now stood directly in front of the phone under surveillance. Two TPF men in uniform, regardless of all subterfuge, stood beefily in the restaurant doorway, hands on hips, and glared out at that subversive telephone.

The voice in Mologna's ear continued, even though everybody in the war room was talking at once. "I said hold *on!*" Mologna yelled into the phone, then yelled at everybody else, "Shut *up*! Tony, saturate that neighborhood! You, tell that phone company to get its head out of its ass and tell me what's goin on. You, tell our people on the scene to close in but stay in character. You, are you recordin this?"

The white male companion of the two black females nodded his earphoned head.

"And are we pickin up a voice from the other end?"

Another nod with earphones.

"Good," Mologna said. "Otherwise, I'd think I was doin a Joan of Arc." Into the phone, he said, "Let me tell you somethin, smart boy."

"I thought maybe we could nego—"

"Just shut up and listen to me. Negotiate with you?" Cappelletti tapped Mologna's shoulder, but Mologna angrily shrugged him away. "Deal with you, you son of a bitch? I wouldn't disgrace my vocal cords doin deals with you." Cappelletti tapped Mologna's shoulder more urgently, and this time Mologna swung his arm around to shove the other man away, meantime yelling into the phone, "I'm goin to get you, you wise-ass bastard, and let me tell you this. When I get my hands on you, you'll fall downstairs for a month!" Slamming the phone down into its cradle, ignoring the voice's feeble, "But—" Mologna spun around to glare at Cappelletti: "And what did *you* want to say, that couldn't wait?"

Cappelletti sighed: "Keep him on the line," he said.

30

"You see," Andy Kelp had explained to Dortmunder before the event, "with the phone company's own phone-ahead gizmo, you have to use their equipment and go through the operator every time you want to use it. But this one is from West Germany—see what it says on the bottom?—and with this one you just set these dials here to the number where you're gonna be, you plug it into the jack where your phone line goes, then plug the phone in on the other side here, and it does the phone-ahead thing without bothering the operator or anybody at all."

"But," Dortmunder had pointed out, "pay phones don't have jacks."

"They got a phone line coming in. And *this* gizmo, made in Japan, these little prongs squeeze down into the line and make contact, so you can set up a jack anywhere you want on any phone line in the city."

"It sounds awful chancy," Dortmunder had said. "Where do we make this thing phone ahead *to*?"

"Another pay phone."

"Fine," Dortmunder had said. "So I'm standing there at this second pay phone, and one of the bozos they've got on stakeout reads the phone-ahead number on the little Kraut gizmo you've got stuck into your little Jap gizmo stuck into the first pay phone, and then they come to phone number two and they arrest me. And probably, because they're a little annoyed at all the trouble they're going through, they have to work very hard to subdue me."

"Well, no," Kelp had said. "Because you aren't going to be at that second pay phone either."

"I'm going crazy," Dortmunder had said. "Where the hell am I, some third pay phone? How many of these phone-ahead gizmos you got?"

"No more pay phones," Kelp had promised. "John, think about the city of New York."

"Why?"

"Because it's our territory, John, so let's use it. And what's one of the main things about this territory?"

"No question-answer," Dortmunder had said, squeezing his beer can so that beer slopped out onto his fingers. "Just tell your story."

"People *move*," Kelp had told him. "They move all the time—uptown, downtown, across town—"

"Outa town."

"Right. And back into town. And every time they move they get a telephone. And they always want it someplace different from the last tenant. Not the kitchen, the bedroom. Not the living room, the—"

"Okay, okay."

"The point is, this city is overrun with unused telephone lines. You spend a lot of time in back yards and fire escapes yourself, didn't you ever notice all those phone lines?"

"No."

"Well, they're there. So what we do, our *second* pay phone is in Brooklyn. Indoors. In a bar or a drugstore or a hotel lobby, someplace where I can get at the phone line coming in. Then I put another of these Japanese prong gizmos on that line, and I run a line of my own to an unused phone line and from there anywhere in the neighborhood: a basement, a closet, an empty apartment, whatever's handy. And that's where you take the call, on a phone we'll bring in ourselves; so as far as the phone company's concerned that phone doesn't even exist! That second pay phone will ring just once, but your phone'll ring too, and right **away** you answer. Nobody answers a pay phone that rings just once, so you'll have privacy."

Dortmunder had scratched the side of his jaw, frowning deeply. "We're three phones down the line now. Why all the complication?"

"Time. They stake out that first phone. You start to talk, they go crazy. After a while they find my phone-ahead gizmo, maybe you're still on the line, still negotiating. They check with the phone company, they get the address on phone number two, now they got to rush down to Brooklyn, stake it out, approach it very carefully, go crazy all over again. And we're where we can see them, and we got time to end the call and go away before they find the new line leading to the unused line leading to us."

"Christ on a crutch," Dortmunder had said.

"Number A," Kelp had pointed out, "you got no alternative. Number B, this'll work, guaranteed."

And so it did, right on down to the question of negotiation. The phone had rung, just once, and Dortmunder had picked it up and started talking, and he was just getting over his nervousness, sitting there in the for-rent empty apartment over the delicatessen (Pay Phone Inside) on Ocean Bay Boulevard, with Kelp at the front window watching the street for cops, when all of a sudden this guy on the other end of the phone, Maloney, started a lot of yelling and screaming in Dortmunder's ear, culminating in an unnecessarily loud *click*, and then a lot of silence.

"Hello?" Dortmunder said. "Hello?"

Kelp wandered over from the window: "What's wrong?"

"He hung up on me."

"He couldn't." Kelp frowned, gazing into the middle distance. "Could my phone system break down somewhere?"

Dortmunder shook his head, and hung up the phone. "It could," he said, "I know damn well it could, but it didn't. Maloney did it himself. He said he wouldn't deal with me. He said he was gonna catch me, and I was gonna fall downstairs for a month."

"He *said* that?"

"He sounded a lot like Tiny Bulcher, only angry."

Kelp nodded. "It's a challenge," he said. "The good guys against the bad guys, with a challenge and a dare and the gauntlet thrown and all like that. Like in Batman."

"In Batman," Dortmunder pointed out, "the bad guys lose."

Kelp looked at him in astonishment. "*We* aren't the bad guys, John," he said. "We're trying to correct a simple, honest mistake, that's all. We're rescuing the Byzantine Fire for the

American people. *And* the Turkish people. We're the *good* guys."

Dortmunder contemplated that idea.

"Come on," Kelp said. "The bad guys'll show up any minute."

"Right." Dortmunder stood up from the stack of newspapers he'd been using for a chair—the apartment's only furnishing—then looked at the phone on the floor. "What about that?"

Kelp shrugged it off. "A standard desk-type black telephone? Who'd want a thing like that? Wipe off your fingerprints and leave it."

31

Kenneth ("Call me Ken") Albemarle was a Commissioner, it hardly mattered of what. In his calm but successful career he had been, among other things, Commissioner of Public Sanitation in Buffalo, New York; Fire Commissioner in Houston, Texas; Commissioner of Schools in Bismarck, North Dakota; and Water Commissioner in Muscatine, Iowa. He was well qualified to be a Commissioner, with a B.A. in Municipal Administration, an M.S. in Governmental Studies and an M.A. in Public Relations, plus inherent talent and a deep-grained awareness of what the job of Commissioner actually meant. The Commissioner's purpose, he knew, was to calm people down. With his excellent employment history and fine academic background, plus his appearance—at 41 he was trim, dark-haired, and businesslike, showing the relaxed self-assurance of a high school basketball coach with a winning team—Ken Albemarle could calm down a roomful of orang-utans, if necessary, and once or twice he'd proved it.

At the moment he was employed by the City of New York as, um, um, *Police* Commissioner, and right now he was

being called upon to calm down two irate FBI men named
Fracharly and Zeedy, who had entered his office shortly before eleven a.m. and now sat across the desk from him absolutely *ruby* with rage. That is, Fracharly was ruby with rage;
Zeedy appeared to be snowy with shock.

"Chief Inspector Mologna," Ken Albemarle said, nodding his head judiciously and pronouncing the name right,
idly tapping his fingertips on his neat and orderly desktop,
"has been a fine police officer for years and years. In fact, he's
been here longer than I have." (Ken Albemarle had been
New York Police Commissioner for seven months.)

"Perhaps," Fracharly said through clenched teeth, "no
one before this has ever noticed the *Chief Inspector's* incompe-
tential quotient."

"He hung up on the man," Zeedy said, hollow-voiced, as
though he still couldn't believe it.

"Just a moment," Ken Albemarle said. Tapping his intercom, he said, "Miss Friday, would you bring me Chief
Inspector Francis Mologna's file?"

"Yes, sir, Commissioner," the intercom replied, in a tinny
voice.

"It won't be in the file," Fracharly said. "It won't be in
the *fiiiiile*—he just *did* it!"

"Quite so," Ken Albemarle said, tapping his fingertips
together. "If you could give me a little of the background on
this, Mister Fracharly, put me in the pic—"

"Zachary," said Fracharly.

"Beg pardon?"

"The name is *Zachary*, not Fracharly! And it's *Agent*, not
Mister! I am Agent Zachary of the Federal Bureau of Investigation! Here, here—" He clawed for his hip pocket.

"No need, no need," Ken Albemarle assured him. "I've
seen your identification. Sorry to get the name wrong. So
you're Zachary and you're . . . Zeedy?"

"Freedly," said Zeedy.

"Oh, my heaven," Ken Albemarle said, chuckling at
himself. "A Spoonerism. Well, no harm done, I've got it now.
Zachary and Freedly. *Agent* Zachary and *Agent* Freedly."

"That's right," Agent Zachary gritted, still through clenched teeth and rubescent face.

"My favorite Spoonerism," Ken Albemarle said, smiling reminiscently, "because it's an improvement really on the original, is 'flutterby' for 'butterfly.'"

"Commissioner," said Agent Freedly.

"Yes?"

"I don't mean to rush you or anything, Commissioner, but I think Mac here's about to leap at your throat."

Ken Albemarle looked at Agent Zachary and saw it was indeed probable. Time to buckle down and do some major calming. "I see," he said, took a deep breath, and proceeded: "I certainly understand and sympathize with your position, gentlemen, and before we do anything else, please let me assure you right here and now that if there has been the slightest breach of proper police procedure, if Chief Inspector Mologna, whether deliberately or through inadvertence, in any way materially harmed or damaged the case upon which you are all engaged, I will personally not rest until a thorough and painstaking investigation has been made of the entire affair. When I became, uh, Police Commissioner of this fine city, I vowed then, at the time of my investiture in the Mayor's office—that's a photo of the occasion framed there on the wall, with the light glinting off the Mayor's head—that any carelessness or improper procedure or unacceptable behavior which *might* have been tolerated in the past—I'm not saying it was, I'm not competent to judge my predecessors in any way, I'm merely saying *if* there may have been any slackening of standards at any time for whatever reason, that slackening, if it occurred, shall stop and cease and desist as from now. Then. As from then, when I became Commissioner. And if you care to look at the record I have established since that day, gentlemen, I honestly believe you will feel much more relieved in your own minds, convinced that under my charge *fairness* and *competency* and a *thorough airing of all disputes without fear or favor* is the hallmark of—"

"Talat Gorsul!" screamed Agent Zachary.

Ken Albemarle halted and blinked. Was that a war cry?

Were these even FBI men? "I beg your pardon?"

"Talat Gorsul," repeated Agent Zachary, more quietly but panting a bit.

"What Mac means," Agent Freedly explained, reaching over to reassuringly pat his co-agent's near forearm, "is the Turkish Chargé d'Affaires at the United Nations. His name is Talat Gorsul."

"Oh, I see," Ken Albemarle said, though he didn't see at all.

"And he intends," Agent Freedly went on, "according to our information, to give a speech before the UN General Assembly at four o'clock this afternoon, in which he's going to suggest that the United States Government itself engineered the theft of the Byzantine Fire."

Ken Albemarle was completely at sea. "Why?"

"Because he wants to."

"But why, why would the United States Government—"

Agent Freedly shook his head. "Do you want Talat Gorsul's reasoning, Commissioner?"

"On loan only."

"We never intended to give Turkey the Byzantine Fire, and this is our way of reneging on the deal."

"But that's ridiculous," Ken Albemarle said.

"If you'll take a look at the speeches made at the United Nations," Agent Freedly said, "I think you'll find they're mostly ridiculous. But that never stops them from being delivered, translated, printed, and very often believed."

"But we didn't have to make the offer in the first place."

"I don't believe," Agent Freedly said, "Mister Gorsul intends to emphasize that fact in his speech."

"I see. It's simple anti-Americanism."

"Anti-Americanism is never actually *simple*," Agent Freedly said. "When their throats grow parched from calling us names, they pause to drink Coke. But the point is, Gorsul intends to make that speech, and the State Department has informed us it doesn't want the speech made. In the old days, of course, we'd merely have poisoned Gorsul at lunch, but—"

"Poisoned!"

"Not fatally," Agent Freedly said. "We're not barbarians. Just give him a tummyache for a few days. In the current climate, of course, we can't do that. So four o'clock becomes our deadline for recovery of the Byzantine Fire."

"Mo-log-na," said Agent Zachary, slowly and distinctly through those apparently glued-together teeth.

"Exactly," Agent Freedly said. Looking four-square at the Commissioner, he lined it out: "An individual claiming to be in possession of the Byzantine Fire arranged for a telephone call for the purpose of negotiation. He asked to speak specifically to the Chief Inspector. Early in the conversation the Chief Inspector lost his temper and hung up."

"I see," said Ken Albemarle. He was getting a headache. "Did the, um, negotiator call back?"

"No."

"Did he appear to be genuine?"

"From the little bit we have of him on tape, yes."

"I see." Ken Albemarle fiddled with the corner of his desk blotter. "Of course, I haven't as yet heard all sides of the matter, but from what you tell me there certainly—"

An interruption entered at that point, in the person of a young woman dressed in black ballet slippers, extremely baggy men's trousers, a very wrinkled white shirt, a *narrow* maroon necktie, an off-white bandleader's jacket six sizes too large for her, and a pair of blue-framed harlequin glasses with rhinestones. This maiden placed a thick dossier on Ken Albemarle's desk, saying, "I'm sorry it took so long, Commissioner, but his name, the spelling, we just . . ."

"That's perfectly all right, Miss Friday. Better late than never. Thank you very much."

"Thank *you*, sir."

Miss Friday, successfully calmed, returned to her own office, while Ken Albemarle leafed quickly through Chief Inspector Francis Mologna's files, picking up a few of the highlights, getting a general impression of the man. And what a lot of skating on thin ice the old boy'd done over the years! Right to the edge *here*, almost tripped up *there*. These old bull elephants, Ken Albemarle knew, if they survived at all, they

knew all the tricks in the world, plus a few extra all their own.
He visualized himself trying, seven months into this job, to
bring down Chief Inspector Mologna at the behest of two
out-of-town FBI men. "Well, well, well," he said. Giving the
out-of-towners his most straightforward look, he said, "I want
you to know I take this matter with the utmost seriousness,
gentlemen. Now, please, I want to hear *all* the details, and
then we'll decide what's best to do for the future."

32

When Dortmunder got back to the apartment, trailed by
Kelp, May was still there. "I thought," Dortmunder said,
"you had work today."

"I called in semisick."

"Semisick?"

"I said if I felt better later I'd come in. I wanted to know
how things went—so how'd things go?"

Dortmunder said, "Is it too early to drink bourbon?"

"It isn't even noon."

"Add a little water."

Kelp said, "May, things didn't go so good. Whyn't I get
us all some beers while John tells you the story?"

"Bourbon," Dortmunder said.

"You don't want bourbon," Kelp told him. "It'd just depress you."

Dortmunder looked at him. "Bourbon would depress
me? *Bourbon* would depress me?" But Kelp, as though Dortmunder hadn't spoken at all, walked on out of the room,
toward the kitchen.

May said, "Sit down, John, tell me about it."

Dortmunder sat down, his knobby elbows on his knobby
knees. "What happened was," he said, "they won't negotiate."

"But you don't want to negotiate. You just want to give it back."

"I didn't get a chance to say so. They hung up on me."

"The *police*?"

"They'd rather catch me," Dortmunder said gloomily, and Kelp came back in with three beers.

May sipped hers through the side of her mouth away from the dangling cigarette, then said, "How did you phrase yourself, John? You weren't arrogant or anything, were you?"

Dortmunder merely looked at her, while Kelp said, "May, I was right there. John was perfect courtesy. In fact, I thought he went too far. He bent over backward, he said he just wanted to *give* the thing back."

"They wouldn't listen," Dortmunder said. "They said they were gonna catch me and I'd fall downstairs for a month."

"Wow," said May.

"That's a terrible threat, May, from a cop," Dortmunder said. "You ever see their new building, downtown? Till now, in a precinct, it's at the most down one metal flight in the back of the place, you just keep curled up. That Police Plaza, that's a *skyscraper*. And it's all brick."

"It wasn't a real threat," May assured him. "It was just a figure of speech."

"I heard his voice," Dortmunder said.

Lighting a new cigarette from the ember of the old, May studied both men, then said, "So what do you do now?"

"Find some other way to give it back," Dortmunder said. "Maybe call a newspaper or a TV station, something like that. I don't think there's an insurance company."

"Um," said Kelp.

Dortmunder looked over at his friend, and Kelp seemed very troubled. "I'm not gonna like this," Dortmunder said.

"I been thinking." Kelp scoffed down some beer, then said, "The cops turning you down that way, it knocked the scales off my eyes."

Dortmunder drank beer. "Okay," he said. "Tell me what you see."

"It isn't enough to give it back."

"Whadaya talking about? I give it back, the heat's off, it's all over."

Kelp shook his head. "There's been too much irritation," he said. "Too many noses out of joint, too much commitment. What they want now is *you*."

Dortmunder burped. "Don't say that, Andy."

"I'm sorry, John, it's true."

"Oh, dear," May said. "I think Andy's right."

"Sure I am," Kelp said, but not as though he was glad to be right. "That stone gets turned over to the cops, that might satisfy some folk, maybe satisfy Turkey and the American people, but it wouldn't satisfy the cops, and it wouldn't satisfy Tiny Bulcher or a lot of other guys we both know. Also, I heard at the O.J. there's a religious angle now, there's these religious fanatics also on your trail, and not to convert you. Just getting the stone back won't do it for them, either."

"You're not making me feel better," Dortmunder said.

"I tell you what you got to do, John," Kelp said. "You got to forget the stone for now and get yourself an alibi."

"I don't follow."

"For the boys at the O.J.," Kelp explained. "That gets the specific personal heat off *you*."

Dortmunder shook his head. "No way. We're not talking about the cops here, we're talking about Tiny Bulcher. We're talking about a lot of street people."

"I realize that," Kelp said. "But we can still do an alibi that'll hold up."

Dortmunder frowned at him. "*We?*"

"Sure we," Kelp said, apparently surprised. "We're in this together, aren't we?"

Dortmunder found himself deeply and surprisingly touched. "Andy," he said, "I don't know what to say."

"That's right," Kelp said, misunderstanding. "So we'll work out what you say."

"No, I mean—I mean that's a terrific offer, but you shouldn't stick your neck out for me."

"Why not? You'd do the same for me, wouldn't you?"

Dortmunder blinked a lot.

Kelp laughed, a trifle shakily. "Sure you would. And the thing of it is, if the three of us all tell the same story—"

"Not May," Dortmunder said.

May said, "John, this is no time for chivalry."

"No," Dortmunder said. "May, in my mind's eye I see Tiny Bulcher biting your nose off, and I don't like it."

"He won't have any reason to bite my nose off," May said, although she did sort of absently touch the part in question. "If we all tell the same story, you won't be under suspicion."

"I won't do it," Dortmunder said. "Not if you're a part of it."

"That's okay," Kelp said. "Two is fine. You and me, we tell the same story, we alibi one another, it works out the same."

Dortmunder considered being chivalrous in re Andy as well, but decided one noble gesture per customer per day was enough. "What alibi?" he asked.

"Well," Kelp said, "I've already mentioned to some of the guys my own alibi, in a general kind of way, so we just fit you in with me."

"What's *your* alibi?"

"The funny thing is, it's the truth. I was at home all that night, doing things with telephones."

"Alone?"

"Yeah."

"Then how does that alibi you?"

"Well," Kelp said, "I made and received a lot of calls. You know? I'd put some gizmo on, I'd want to try it, I'd call somebody. If it was my answering machine or my call-waiting gadget or something like that, I'd call somebody and have them call me back."

"Right," Dortmunder said. "So all night you're covered, on account of these phone calls."

"Sure. And now I say you were with me, helping me like with the wiring, and now we're both covered."

Dortmunder said, "How come you didn't mention before

about me being there? Like when you told people your alibi. Or like when you were making all these calls Wednesday night."

"The question didn't come up."

"I don't know," Dortmunder said.

May said, "John, this is a wonderful gesture on Andy's part, and the fact of the matter is, you're in no position to look wonderful gestures in the mouth."

Dortmunder drank beer.

Kelp said, "We'll go back to my place, I'll give you half an hour instruction on telephones, you'll know as much as I do. Then it's our hobby together."

"If it goes wrong," Dortmunder pointed out, "Tiny won't like you any more either."

Kelp waved that away with an airy sweep of his beer can: "How could it go wrong?" he asked.

33

"He annoyed me," Mologna said to Leon. "I was gettin all this shit about telephones—he is there, he isn't there, it's goin through, it isn't goin through—and I just forgot myself."

"This too will pass," Leon said, his face a woodcut entitled *Sympathy*. He was feeling so bad on Mologna's account that he wasn't even dancing in place.

Mologna sat slumped at his desk, forearms sprawled among his papers. "The static I'm goin to take," he said, shaking his heavy head. "The static I am goin to take."

It had already started. The Commissioner—Mologna could never remember the man's name, and didn't see any real reason to make the effort—had called to chew him out in that discreet, distant, with-gloves-on manner of upper-echelon bureaucrats everywhere. The point, as Mologna well knew, was not what the Commissioner said, or what he himself said in response; the point was that in the Commissioner's phone log and in his day book and in Mologna's personal file there would now be a notation to the effect that the Commissioner had demonstrated leadership. The son of a bitch.

Well, maybe not entirely a son of a bitch at that, since the Commissioner had in the same phone call made it very clear where Mologna's true enemies were: "FBI Agents Zachary and Freedly are in my office at this very moment, discussing the situation with me," the Commissioner had said, and the background gasp of outraged betrayal behind the Commissioner's voice had been the only bright spot in that entire fumigated conversation.

Was there anything to be done about Zachary and Freedly? Was there anything to be done to protect his own ass, now that he'd exposed it for all the world to see?

The only real solution, obviously, was to *find that goddam ruby*. And to find it *with* perpetrator; this wasn't the kind of little trouble that could be smoothed over with a nice piece of jewelry. What the public would need this time, what the Police Department and the FBI and the State Department and the United Nations and the Turkish Government would need, what Mologna himself would need, was a human sacrifice. Nothing less. "We've got to get him," Mologna said aloud.

"Oh, I couldn't agree more," Leon said. He and Mologna were alone in Mologna's big office in Police Plaza, partly because Mologna wanted it that way and partly because right at the moment nobody else in the great city of New York wanted to be linked with Francis Mologna in any way.

"And *we've* got to get him," Mologna went on. "Not the fuckin FBI, or any a them foreign bozos."

"Oh, absolutely."

"And not the goddam criminal element either. Though the bleedin Christ knows, they've got the best shot at it."

"Unfortunate," Leon said. "If only our man were gay, I might be able to do some undercover work myself."

Mologna squinted at him. "Leon," he said, "I'm never entirely sure when you're bein obscene."

Leon pressed graceful fingertips to his narrow chest.
"*Me?*"

"In any case," Mologna said, "you heard the tape. Did
that sound like a goddam faggot to you?"

"If he is," Leon said, "he's so far back in the closet he
must poop mothballs."

"You're disgustin, Leon." Briefly, Mologna brooded.
"The criminal element," he said. "What happens if they find
him first?"

"They turn him over to us. With the Byzantine Fire, of
course."

"Maybe. Maybe." Mologna squinted at the far wall, trying to see into the future. "Maybe the press gets onto it first?
Maybe the word gets out the crooks helped us do our own
job? Not good, Leon."

"Ungood all the way."

"That's right." With sudden decision, Mologna said,
"Leon, call Tony Cappelletti, have him reel in that stoolie of
his, Whatsisname."

"Benjamin Arthur Klopzik."

"Like I said. I want Tony to wire him, full radio pickup. I
want to know every word said in that thieves' den of theirs
before they know it themselves. And I want every available
TPF man in the city at the ready, no more than three blocks
from that saloon. If and when those boyos find our man, I
want to take him away from them *that second*."

"Oh, very good," Leon said. "Incisive, decisive, and oh so
correct."

"Give me the bullshit later," Mologna told him. "First
make the phone call."

34

The back room at the O.J. looked like one of those paintings
from the Russian Revolution—the storming of the Winter

Palace—or, perhaps more appropriately, from the Revolution of the French: a Jacobin trial during the Terror. The place had never been so crowded, so smoky, so hot, so full of strife and contention. Tiny Bulcher and three assistant judges sat together on one side of the round card table, facing the door, with several other tough guys ranged behind them, on their feet, leaning against the stacked liquor cartons. A few more savage-looking types lurked to both sides. A couple of chairs had been left empty near the door, facing Tiny and the rest across the green felt table. Harsh illumination from the single hanging bare bulb with its tin reflector in the middle of the room washed out all subtlety of color, reducing the scene to the work of a genre painter with a poor palette, or perhaps a German silent film about Chicago gangsters. Menace and pitiless self-interest glinted on the planes of every face, the slouch of every shoulder, the bend of every knee, the sharpness of every eye, the slant of every smoldering cigarette. Everybody smoked, everybody breathed, and—because it was hot in here—everybody sweated. Also, when there was no one being interviewed everybody talked at once, except when Tiny Bulcher wanted to make a general point, at which time he would thump the table with fist and forearm, bellow, "Shadap!" and insert a sentence into the resulting silence.

It was, in short, a scene to make even the innocent pause, had there been any innocents around to glom it. Dortmunder, of the guilty the most singularly guilty, was very lucky he had to cool his heels in the outer brightness of the bar long enough to knock back two double bourbons on the rocks before it became his and Kelp's turn to enter that back room and face all those cold eyes.

The way they were called in, a fellow they knew slightly, named Gus Brock, came to the table out front where they were waiting, and said, "Hello, Dortmunder, Kelp."

"Hiya, Gus," Kelp said. Dortmunder just nodded; he was going for dignity.

"You guys are a team, right?"

"Right!" said Kelp.

"You're next," Gus Brock said. "Lemme give you the layout. This isn't the law, we're not out to screw anybody or trap anybody. What happens, you guys go in, you stand just inside the door, you'll listen to the guy ahead of you, that way you know the routine when it's your turn. Right?"

"Very fair," Kelp said. "That's really very fair, Gus."

Ignoring him, Gus glanced up as a very pale and nervous-looking guy came out from the back, tottered to the bar, and said hoarsely, "Rye. Leave the bottle."

Gus nodded. "Let's go."

So they went, and when they walked into the smoky, glary, stinking back room full of all that potential violence and destruction, Dortmunder reconsidered his life from the very beginning: *could* he have made it as a supermarket clerk? By now he'd be maybe an assistant manager, out in the suburbs maybe, with a black bow tie. The prospect had never pleased before, but with this alternative staring him in the face there was certainly something to be said for a life in a clean well-lighted place.

Everybody was talking, even arguing, except for a stout, sweating man with a bald spot, who was seated in one of the chairs facing the court, mopping his face and forearms and baldness with an already-drenched white handkerchief. Dortmunder, trying to remember how to keep his knees locked, faintly heard Kelp, under the din, ask, "Who's those guys over on the right?"

"Representatives from the Terrorists' Cooperative," Gus Brock said.

Dortmunder leaned back against the wall, while Kelp said, "Terrorists' Cooperative?"

"There's a lot of these foreign bunches interested," Gus Brock explained. "They're looking for the same thing as us, and they all combined together to help each other. And now they're combined with us. They're looking around among their local ethnics."

"Boy," said Kelp, with what struck Dortmunder as obscene enthusiasm. "What a manhunt!"

"You bet," Gus Brock said. "The son of a bitch doesn't have a chance."

Whomp, went Tiny Bulcher's fist and forearm: "Shadap!"

Silence.

Tiny smiled like a shark at the fat man in the witness chair. "What's your name, guy?"

"Hah—hah—kuh, kuh, uhh, Harry," said the fat man. "Harry Matlock."

"Harry Matlock," Tiny said, looking to his left, and one of the standing men poked around among a lot of folders and envelopes stuck in among the liquor cartons, finally bringing out a small used brown envelope from the phone company, which he handed to the guy to Tiny's left, who pulled several wrinkled scraps of paper out of the envelope, smoothed them on the felt, and nodded his readiness. Then Tiny said, "Tell us your story, Harry. Where were you at midnight Wednesday?"

The fat man swabbed his neck and said, "Muh-me and three other guys—"

The door opened, whacking Dortmunder on the shoulder blades. He leaned out of the way, looking back, and saw Benjy Klopzik scooting in. "Sorry," Benjy whispered.

Tiny Bulcher yelled past the fat man, "Benjy! Where you been?"

"Hi, Tiny," the little man said, shutting the door behind himself. "I hadda feed my dog."

"Whadayou doin with a dog? Stand in that corner, I'll take you for a walk later." Switching his glare to the fat man, he said, "So? Whadja stop for?"

Benjy inserted himself delicately under the elbows of the Terrorists' Cooperative. The fat man swabbed himself all over and said, "I was in Huntington, Long Island. Me and three other guys. We were taking out an antique store."

"Antiques? Old furniture?"

"Valuable stuff," the fat man said. "We had a purchaser and everything, a dealer downtown on Broadway." Shaking his damp head, he said, "It all fell through, on accounta the blitz. We couldn't make delivery Thursday, then the cops found the truck."

"This is Long Island," the man to the left of Tiny said. "Kennedy fucking Airport's on Long Island."

"We were way to hell and gone," the fat man said desperately, bouncing wetly around on his chair. "Honest. Huntington, Long Island, it's way out on the island, it's way up on the North Shore."

Tiny said, "Who were these other three guys?"

"Ralph Demrovsky, Willy Car—"

"One at a time!"

"Oh," the fat man said. "Sorry."

Tiny had looked around at one of the standing men to his right. "We got Demrovsky?"

"I'm looking."

Now Dortmunder saw that in fact a rough-and-ready sort of filing system had been created back there, with folders and envelopes stuck in among the floor-to-ceiling liquor cartons. Apparently, each guy standing back there had a separate part of the alphabet to deal with. Education, Dortmunder thought, is a wonderful thing.

"Here it is."

The file this time was in a small folded restaurant menu. This was handed to the man seated at Tiny's right, who opened it, leafed through the few ratty papers in it, and said, "Yeah, we talked to him already. Gave the same story."

Tiny looked at the fat man. "What time'd you get to this antique store?"

"Eleven-thirty."

The man with the fat man's file made a note. Tiny lifted an eyebrow at the man with Demrovsky's file, who nodded agreement. Then Tiny looked back at the fat man: "What time'd you leave?"

"Three o'clock."

"Demrovsky," said the other guy, "says two-thirty."

"It was around there," the fat man said, sounding panicky. "Who's looking at their watch? It was around two-thirty, three o'clock."

Dortmunder closed his eyes. The questioning went on, bringing out the other two names, comparing everybody's story with everybody else. The fat man was innocent, at least of stealing the Byzantine Fire, and soon everybody in the room knew it, so the last part of the questioning was merely to double-check the alibis of other people. *I'm next*, Dortmunder thought, and the thought was barely complete when the fat man was dismissed, patting and swabbing himself and hurrying from the room, leaving his seat for Dortmunder, who tottered to it, grateful at least to be seated, not entirely sure he was grateful to have Kelp seated beside him. The door behind him opened and closed, but Dortmunder didn't look back to see who was now on deck.

"So," Tiny Bulcher said. "You two guys were together Wednesday night."

"That's right," Kelp said, speaking right up. "We were working on my phones."

"Tell us about it," Tiny offered, and Kelp did, reeling off the story they'd cooked up together, rattling right along, putting in all the details, while Dortmunder sat beside him, silent and dignified and scared shitless.

Early on in the questioning, already existing files (Kelp's in a Valentine's Day card, Dortmunder's in a thin cardboard packet that had originally contained bunion pads) were brought out, checked, annotated. Dortmunder moodily watched the guy with his file, wondering what was already written down on those odds and ends of paper, what facts, clues, hints, suggestions, information was waiting in there to trip him up. Something, something.

Tiny and the guy with Kelp's folder asked a few questions, in a not particularly threatening manner, and it became clear that one or two of Kelp's phone pals of Wednesday night had already mentioned his calls. But then, after the deceptive calm, Tiny's ball-bearing eyes rolled infinitesimally in their sockets, and there he was looking at Dortmunder and saying, "So you were with him, right?"

"That's right," Dortmunder said.

"All night."

"Oh, yeah. Oh, yeah."

Kelp said, "John helped me with the wir—"

"Shadap."

"Okay."

Tiny nodded slowly, looking at Dortmunder. "You call anybody?"

"No," Dortmunder said.

"How come?"

"Well, uh, it was Andy's phone. And my woman was at the movies."

Continuing to gaze at Dortmunder, Tiny asked his assistants generally, "Kelp mention Dortmunder to anybody?"

"No," they all said.

"Well," Kelp said.

"Shadap."

"Okay."

The guy with Dortmunder's file said, "You went to see Arnie Albright Thursday."

Oh, no. God, let it be not so. I'll be good. I'll get a Social Security card. A real one. "Yeah, I did," Dortmunder said.

"You told him you made a score."

"Tuesday," Dortmunder said. Unfortunately, his voice squeaked on the first syllable.

"But you went to Arnie Thursday," the guy said. "And you were looking up another fence, name of Stoon, the same day."

"That's right."

"You had some stuff to sell."

"That's right."

"What stuff?"

"Um . . . jewelry."

General alertness animated the room. Tiny said, "You did a jewelry heist? Wednesday night?"

"No," Dortmunder said. "Tuesday night."

A terrorist said, "Where?"

"Staten (cough) Staten Island."

The guy with Dortmunder's file said, "What fences did you see Wednesday?"

"Nobody," Dortmunder said. "I was kind of sick Wednesday. It was raining Tuesday night—" (it's always good to throw a little truth into a story, like adding salt to a recipe) "—and I got like a cold. Just one of those twenty-four-hour bugs."

Another guy said, "Where in Staten Island?"

"On Drumgoole Boulevard. It didn't make the papers."

One of the terrorists said, "What did you rob?"

Dortmunder looked at him, wondering if he was one of the religious fanatics. "Just some engagement rings, watches, stuff like that. Ordinary stuff."

Tiny said, "What fence did you sell it to?"

"I didn't," Dortmunder said. "I couldn't. The blitz came along, and—"

"So you've still got the stash."

Dortmunder hadn't been ready for that one. In the millionth of a second which was the only delay he dared offer, he considered the alternatives: Say no, and they'll wonder why he got rid of a perfectly ordinary jewelry haul which could be hidden a thousand different places until the blitz was over. Say yes, and they'll want to see it. "Yes," Dortmunder said.

Tiny said, "Dortmunder, we know each other a while."

"Sure."

"There's a stink coming off you, Dortmunder. I never smelled it before."

"I'm nervous, Tiny."

"We'll look at your stash," Tiny said. "We'll send six guys with you, and—"

"*Breaker! Breaker!*" said a loud metallic voice, everywhere in the room.

Tiny frowned around, this way and that: "What?"

"*I don't care about that,*" said the loud metallic voice.

Seven or eight people in the room spoke at once. Then the loud metallic voice spoke over all of them, saying, "*Well, I'm stuck here on West End Avenue with a busted transmission and I want to talk to my wife in Englewood, New Jersey.*"

"A radio," said a terrorist.

"CB," said one of Tiny's co-judges.

"Wire," Tiny said. His eyebrows were lowering practically to his upper lip. "Some dirty son of a bitch bastard in this room is wired, is bugging us, is—"

"*Because,*" said the loud metallic voice in deep exasperation, "*my wife is listening on this channel.*"

A terrorist said, "His equipment is picking up these CB

signals. A similar terrible thing happened to a late acquaintance of mine in Basra."

"*I'll report you,*" yelled the loud metallic voice, "*to the FCC, that's what I'll do, you filthy air-hog!*"

"Who," said Tiny, flexing many of his muscles. "Who."

People looked this way and that, wide-eyed, listening for the return of the loud metallic voice.

"*If I could get my hands on you—*"

"BENJY!"

The little man was already halfway to the door. Bouncing off a terrorist's chest, ducking under a tough guy's clutching hands, he shot from the room like a freed parakeet.

Naturally, Dortmunder and Kelp joined in the chase.

35

Talat Gorsul, Turkish Chargé d'Affaires at the United Nations, a sleek, smooth, swarthy, heavy-lidded man with a nose like a coat hanger, emerged from his limousine and paused, his opaque eyes taking in the upright brick finger of Police Headquarters in Police Plaza. "Only a nation with no sense of history," he said, in his velvety uninflected voice, "would build a police headquarters that looks like the Bastille."

His aide, a stocky spy named Sanli, a man who perspired a lot and never shaved very well, snickered. It was a major part of his job at the UN to snicker at Talat Gorsul's asides.

"Ah, well," Gorsul said. "Wait," he told the driver, and, "Come," he told Sanli. He that he told to wait, waited, and he that he told to come, came. They crossed the brick forecourt to the brick building, went through the security check in the main lobby, and rode up in the elevator to a high floor, where they passed a second security check and at last entered a conference room packed with people, half of them in uniform.

At the last such meeting of these people in this room, Gorsul had sent Sanli. Now, he nodded noncommittally as Sanli introduced him to a man named Zachary, from the Federal Bureau of Investigation, who in turn introduced him to everybody else: police officials, government officials, even an assistant district attorney, though there was hardly anyone at this point to prosecute.

The introductions complete, Talat Gorsul sat for the next fifteen minutes at the foot of the conference table, smooth-faced, heavy-lidded, and unemotional, while he listened to several reams of platitude, jargon, and cant from one after the other of those present: the steps that were being taken, the plans for recovery of the Byzantine Fire, the increased security already laid on for after the Byzantine Fire had been found, on and on and on. At the end of it all, Zachary from the FBI rose to say, "Mister Gorsul, I hope and trust this display of our determinativeness has convinced you of our sincerability." To the room at large, Zachary explained (as though it were necessary), "Mister Gorsul has been considerating an address to the United Nations with the implicatory thrust that we might for some reason be in a foot-dragging posture on this investigatory situation."

Smoothly but promptly Gorsul was on his feet. "I do appreciate, Mister Zachary," he said, "your interpreting me for all these industrious professional persons, but if I may make the slightest correction to the general line of your statement, please permit me to assure all of you ladies and gentlemen that neither in my heart nor on my lips have I ever had the slightest doubt as to your professionalism, your dedication, or your loyalty to your own national government. The questions I intend to raise this afternoon at the United Nations are most certainly not intended to cast doubt upon any of you in this room. No, nor to cast doubt anywhere at all, come to that. I shall wonder, a bit later today at the United Nations, how such a security-conscious nation as this—I was, by the by, impressed with the two layers of security through which I passed on my way in here—how such a security-conscious nation as the United States, so large, so powerful, so experienced in these matters, could have permitted this admittedly minor bauble to slip through its all-powerful fingers in the first place. A small question, a matter of personal curiosity only, which I intend, somewhat later today, to share with my colleagues at the United Nations."

"Mister Gorsul."

Gorsul looked toward the voice, seeing a blue-uniformed stout man with a storm-tossed face. "Yes?"

"I'm Chief Inspector Francis X. Maloney," the stout man said, heaving himself to his feet. (Mologna, Gorsul remembered.)

"Ah, yes. We were introduced, Chief Inspector Mologna."

Plodding steadily around the conference table toward the door, his round belly leading the way, Mologna said, "I wonder if you and I could have a word or two in private, if all these other leaders of men would excuse us."

There was general surprise, some consternation, some murmuring. The FBI man, Zachary, seemed inclined to put his oar in, but Mologna fixed Gorsul with a meaningful stare (but with what meaning?) and said, "It's up to you, Mister Gorsul. I think it's to your own best interest."

"If it is to my nation's best interest," Gorsul responded, "of course I shall accede to your request."

"That's all right, then," Mologna said, opened the hall door, and stood to one side.

It wasn't often that Talat Gorsul faced the unexpected; it was in fact a part of his job never to place himself in a situation where he wasn't reasonably sure what would happen next. It was the piquancy of this development, then, as much as any profit that might ensue from a private conversation with Mologna, that led him to say to the table at large, "If you will all excuse me?" Getting to his feet, he walked to the door and preceded Mologna out to the hall.

Where Mologna smiled at the two uniformed city policemen on guard duty and genially told them, "That's okay, boys, take a walk down the corridor."

The boys took a walk down the corridor, and Mologna

turned toward Gorsul. "Well, Mister Gorsul," he said, "so you live on Sutton Place."

This was *really* unexpected. "Yes, I do."

"The car in which you're normally chauffeured is license number DPL 767," Mologna went on, "and the car you drive for yourself when you go out of town on weekends, here and there, that's DPL 299."

"Both are Mission cars, not mine," Gorsul pointed out.

"That's right. Mister Gorsul, you're a diplomat. I'm not. You're an oily son of a bitch Turk, I'm a blunt Irishman. Don't make any speeches this afternoon."

Gorsul stared at him in utter astonishment. "Are you *threatening* me?"

"You're damn right I am," Mologna said, "and what are you goin to do about it? Over there at that Mission of yours you got a dozen chauffeurs and secretaries and cooks. I got fifteen thousand men, Mister Gorsul, and do you know what those fifteen thousand men think every time they see a car with diplomat plates parked by a fire hydrant or in a tow-away zone? Do you know what my boys think when they see those DPL plates?"

Gorsul glanced at the two police guards chatting together down at the end of the hall, hands on hips above their guns and gunbelts. He shook his head.

"They're pissed off, Mister Gorsul," Mologna said. "They can't ticket those cars, they can't tow those cars away, they can't even chew out the owners of those cars like a normal citizen. *I wish I could get those sons of bitches*, is what my boys think. You ever been burgled, Mister Gorsul, over there on Sutton Place?"

"No," Gorsul said.

"You're lucky. Lot of burglaries over there. Rich people need a lot of police protection, Mister Gorsul. They need a lot of police *cooperation*. Ever have a motor vehicle accident in the City of New York, Mister Gorsul?"

Gorsul licked thin lips. "No," he said.

"You're a lucky man," Mologna assured him. Then he leaned forward—Gorsul automatically recoiled, then cursed himself for having done so—and more quietly and confidentially he said, "Mister Gorsul, I put my nuts in the wringer on this one, a little earlier today. Normally, I wouldn't give a fuck what you say, what you do, you or anybody else. But just this minute, just today, I can't afford any more shit hittin the fan. You follow me?"

"I might," Gorsul said.

"Good man." Mologna thumped him on the shoulder. "They convinced you in there, right?"

"Yes."

"*They* did, not me. So no speech this afternoon."

Gorsul's heavy-lidded eyes hated, but his mouth said, "That's right."

Another shoulder thump from the detested Mologna's disgusting hand. "That's fine," the rotten Mologna said. "Let's go back in and give those assholes the good news."

36

When May came home from her job at the supermarket, two sacks of groceries in her arms, the phone was ringing. She didn't particularly like events to pile up like that, so she squinted with some alarm and dislike at the ringing monster through the cigarette smoke rising up past her left eye as she dumped the groceries on the sofa. Plucking the final smoldering ember of cigarette from the corner of her mouth and flicking it into a handy ashtray, she picked up the phone and said, with mistrust, "Yes?"

A voice whispered, "May."

"No," she said.

"May?" The voice was still a whisper.

"No obscene calls," May said. "No breathers, none of that. I've got three brothers, they're all big, mean men, they're ex-Marines, they—"

"May!" the voice whispered, shrill and harsh. "It's me! *You* know!"

"And they'll come beat you up," May finished. She hung up, with some sense of satisfaction, and lit a new cigarette.

She was carrying the groceries on into the kitchen when the phone rang again. "Bother," she said, put the sacks on the kitchen table, went back to the living room, picked up the phone, and said, "I warned you once."

"May, it's *me*!" whispered the same voice, loud and desperate. "Don't you recognize me?"

May frowned: "John?"

"Sssssshhhhh!"

"Juh—what happened?"

"Something went wrong. I can't come home."

"Are you at An—"

"Sssssshhhhhhh!"

"Are you at, uh, that place?"

"No. He can't go home either."

"Oh, dear," May said. She had hoped against hope, but she had known this was a possibility.

"We're hiding out," the now-familiar voice whispered.

"Until it blows over?"

"This isn't gonna blow over, May," the voice whispered. "We can't wait that long. This thing's got the staying power of the pyramids."

"What are you going to do?"

"Something," whispered the voice, with a kind of dogged hopelessness.

"Juh—I brought home steak." She moved the phone to her other hand and the cigarette to the other corner of her mouth. "Can I get in touch with you somewhere?"

"No, we're— This phone doesn't have a number."

"Call the operator, she'll tell you."

"No, I don't mean there isn't a number *on* it, I mean it doesn't *have* a number. We plugged into a line. We can dial out, but nobody can call in."

"Does An— Uh. Does he still have that access?"

"Not any more. We took a lot of stuff and left. Listen,

May, somebody may come around. Maybe you oughta go visit your sister."

"I don't really like Cleveland." In truth, May didn't really like her sister.

"Still," the voice whispered.

"We'll see what happens," May promised.

"Still," the voice insisted.

"I'll think about it. You'll call again?"

"Sure."

The doorbell rang.

"There's somebody at the door," May said. "I better get off now."

"Don't answer!"

"They don't want *me*, Juh—I'll just tell them the truth."

"Okay," the voice whispered, but sounded very dubious.

"Be well," May told him, and hung up and went to open the door. Four big burly men—rather similar to May's mental image of her nonexistent ex-Marine brothers—shouldered their way in, saying, "Where is he?"

May shut the door after them. "I don't know any of you people," she said.

"We know you," they said. "Where is he?"

"If you were him," May said, "would you be here?"

"Where *is* he?" they demanded.

"If you were him," May said, "would you tell me where you were?"

They looked at each other, stymied by the truth, and the doorbell rang. "Don't answer it!" they said.

"I answered for you," she pointed out. "This is open house."

The new arrivals were plainclothes detectives, three of them. "Police," they said, showing unnecessary identification.

"Come on in," May said.

The three detectives and the four tough guys looked at each other in the living room. "Well well well," said the detectives. "We're waiting for a friend," said the tough guys. "I've got to unpack my groceries," said May, leaving them to work it out among themselves.

37

"It seems," Mologna said, unsmilingly gazing at Zachary and Freedly, "I was right."

"That may well be," Zachary acknowledged, as brisk and alert as though *he'd* been right. "We'll know more, of course, once we've interrogated this individual."

"Dortmunder," Mologna said, tapping the dossier Leon had lovingly placed in the exact center of his desk. "John Archibald Dortmunder. Born in Dead Indian, Illinois, raised in the Bleedin Heart Sisters of Eternal Misery Orphanage, thousands of arrests on suspicion of robbery, two jail terms. Hasn't been heard from recently, but that doesn't mean he isn't active. An ordinary, home-grown, minor-league, light-fingered crook. Not an international spy, not a terrorist, not a freedom fighter, not a political in any way." A quick glance at Freedly: "Not even an Armenian." Back to Zachary, the chief asshole: "A small-time crook, all on his own. Pulled a small-time jewelry store burglary, got the Byzantine Fire by mistake. Like I said all along."

"It's very possible you're right," Zachary said. "Of course, under interrogation it may well turn out this man Dortmunder has been recruited by some other element."

Freedly said, "And then there's his partner, Kelp."

"Andrew Octavian Kelp," Mologna said, his fingertips sensing that second dossier beneath the first. "Dortmunder's partner in his alibi, but not in the heist. I assume Dortmunder has somethin on Kelp and forced him into supportin that alibi. Kelp himself is absolutely clean the night of the robbery."

"Could be the link," Freedly said.

Zachary frowned at him: "What?"

"If there is a link," Mologna acknowledged, "which I very much doubt."

Zachary said, "What?"

"It's *Kelp's* foreign associations we'll have to check into," Freedly said, making a note.

Zachary said, "Goddam it."

"Link between Dortmunder and international aspect,"
Freedly explained.

"Oh, *Kelp*!" Zachary said, and immediately leaped on
the idea and rode madly off in all directions. "Excellent concept! 'Kelp, Kelp'—the name is obviously shortened. He'll
have relatives in the old country. *He's* establishing the alibi
while Dortmunder's out pulling the actual job. Ruby-
Oswald!"

"They weren't linked," Mologna pointed out.

"Concept," Zachary explained. "In the theorizational
stage, many linkages were postulated between those two.
While they all turned out to be inappropriate in that instance, some of the same theories could very well come into
play in this situation."

"Why not," Mologna said. "They'll work just as well as
last time." He looked up as the door opened: "Yes, Leon?"

"Captain Cappelletti," Leon announced. "With that
cute little tattletale."

"Let's see them," Mologna said, and Leon ushered in
Tony Cappelletti, shooing ahead of himself Benjamin Arthur
Klopzik.

Who was a changed man. Absolute terror had made him
even thinner than before, but with a wiry, tensile strength
that was very new. He was still scrawny but, on looking at
him, one felt he might be able, like an ant, to lift and carry a
crumb seven times his weight. His huge hollow eyes darted
this way and that, as though expecting Mologna's office to be
full of his former comrades; they lit with horror and wild
surmise when they met the curious gazes of Zachary and
Freedly. "Ak!" he said, recoiling into Tony Cappelletti's chest.

"These are FBI men, Klopzik," Mologna said. "Agents
Zachary and Freedly. Come on in here and quit foolin
around."

Hesitantly, Klopzik advanced far enough into the room
for Cappelletti also to enter and Leon to shut the door behind
them. Then Klopzik stopped and merely waited, blinking.

"You did fine," Mologna told him. "We picked up every
word. It wasn't your fault about that goddam CB. You may

be happy to hear we towed that son of a bitch's car away *and* slapped a reckless drivin charge on him, just to relieve our feelins."

"They're gonna kill me." Klopzik's voice sounded like a zipper opening.

"No, they won't, Benjy," Cappelletti said, and told Mologna, "I promised him the protection of the Department."

"Well, sure," Mologna said.

"But this time," Cappelletti said, "we really got to do it."

Mologna frowned. "What are you tellin me, Tony?"

"This time," Cappelletti explained, "we don't have just one mob or half a dozen ex-partners looking for a guy. Every professional crook in New York is looking for Benjy Klopzik." (Klopzik groaned.) "If they find him, they'll never trust the Police Department again."

"Ah," Mologna said. "I see what you mean."

Zachary, sitting firmly like an FBI man, said, "Of course, the Bureau has considerable experiential knowledge in this sort of area: new identities, jobs, a new life in a completely different part of the country. We could—"

"No!" cried Klopzik.

Mologna looked at him. "You don't want help?"

"Not from the FBI! That program of theirs, that's just a delay of sentence! Everybody the FBI gives a new identity, the first thing you know the guy's been buried under the new name."

"Oh, now," Zachary said, offended on the Bureau's behalf. "I'll admit we've had a few problems from time to time, but there's no point overstating the case."

Mologna shook his head, seeing from Klopzik's anguished face that the little man would not be dissuaded. "All right, Klopzik," he said. "What do you want?"

"I don't wanna move out of New York," Klopzik said, his terror receding. "What are all those other places to me? They don't even have the subway."

"What do you *want*?"

"Plastic surgery," Klopzik said, so promptly that it was clear he'd been thinking about this rather intently. "And a new name, a new identity—driver's license and all that. And a nice soft job with decent money and not much to do—maybe in the Parks Department. And I can't go back to my old place, so I need a nice rent-controlled apartment and new furniture and a color TV . . . and a dishwasher!"

"Klopzik," Mologna said, "you want to stay in New York? Right here where they're lookin for you?"

"Sure, Francis," Cappelletti said. "I think it's an okay idea. This is the last place in the world they'll expect to find him. Anywhere else, he'll stick out like a sore thumb."

"He *is* a sore thumb," Mologna said.

"I was kinda thinking about making a change anyway," Klopzik confided to the room at large. "Things were kinda getting out of hand."

Mologna considered him. "Is that all?"

"Yeah," Klopzik said. "Only, I don't wanna be a Benjy any more."

"Yeah?"

"Yeah. I wanna be a, a . . . *Craig!*"

Mologna sighed. "Craig," he said.

"Yeah." Klopzik actually grinned. "Craig Fitzgibbons," he said.

Mologna looked at Tony Cappelletti. "Take Mister Fitzgibbons outa here," he said.

"Come along, Benjy."

"And, and," Klopzik said, resisting Cappelletti's tugging hand, staring with wild-eyed hope at Mologna, getting it *all* out, the whole big, beautiful, suddenly-realizable dream, "and tell the plastic surgeon I wanna look like, like *Dustin Hoffman!*"

"Get it outa here," Mologna told Tony Cappelletti, "or I'll start the plastic surgery right now."

But that was all; Klopzik had shot his wad. Exhausted, satiated, happy, he allowed himself to be led away.

In the silence following upon Klopzik/Fitzgibbons' departure, Mologna looked bleakly at Zachary and Freedly and said, "That Dortmunder's got a lot to answer for."

"I'm looking forward to questioning him," Zachary said, getting the implication wrong.

"Oh, so am I," Mologna said.

Freedly said, "There isn't any doubt, is there, Chief Inspector?"

Mologna frowned at him. "Doubt? Dortmunder did it, all right. There's no doubt."

"No, I mean that we'll get him."

Mologna's heavy mouth opened in a slow smile. "At a rough estimate," he said, "I would guess there are currently four hundred thousand men, women, and children in the City of New York looking for John Archibald Dortmunder. Don't worry, Mister Freedly, we'll get him."

38

"I'm a dead man," Dortmunder said.

"Always the pessimist," Kelp said.

Around them hummed thousands—no, millions—of silent conversations, whistling and whispering through the cables; unfaithful husbands making assignations all unknowingly a millimicrometer away from their all-unknowing faithless wives; business deals being closed an eyelash distance from the unsuspecting subjects who'd be ruined by them; truth and lies flashing along cheek by jowl in parallel lanes, never meeting; love and business, play and torment, hope and the end of hope all spun together inside the cables from the teeming telephones of Manhattan. But of all those chattering voices Dortmunder and Kelp heard nothing—only the distant, arrhythmic plink of dripping water.

They were truly under the city now, burrowed down so far beneath the towers that the occasional rumble of a nearby subway seemed to come from *above* them. The hunted man, like the hunted animal, when he goes to ground goes under the ground.

Beneath the City of New York squats another city,

mostly nasty, brutish, and short. And dark, and generally wet. The crisscrossing tunnels carry subway trains, commuter trains, long-distance trains, city water, city sewage, steam, electric lines, telephone lines, natural gas, gasoline, oil, automobiles, and pedestrians. During Prohibition a tunnel from the Bronx to northern Manhattan carried beer. The caverns beneath the city store wine, business records, weapons, Civil Defense equipment, automobiles, building supplies, dynamos, money, water, and gin. Through and around the tunnels and the caverns trickle the remnants of the ancient streams the Indians fished when Manhattan Island was still a part of nature. (As late as 1948, a bone-white living fish was captured in a run-off beneath the basement of a Third Avenue hardware store. It saw daylight for the first time in the last instant of its life.)

Down into this netherworld Kelp had led Dortmunder, jingling and jangling with his telephones and lines and gizmos, down into an endless round pipe four feet in diameter, running away to infinity in both directions, coated with phone cables but at least dry and equipped with electric lights at regular intervals. One couldn't stand upright but could sit with some degree of comfort. An adapter on one of the light sockets now serviced an electric heater, so they were warm. After a few errors—disconnecting and disconcerting several thousand callers, who naturally blamed the phone company—Kelp had rigged up a telephone of their own, so they could make contact with the city above. Dortmunder'd made the first call, to May, and Kelp had made the second, to a pizza place that made deliveries—though it had taken a while to convince them to make such a delivery to a street corner. Kelp had persevered, however, and at the agreed-on time had scurried up to ground level, returning with pizza and beer and a newspaper and word that the sky was overcast: "Looks like rain."

So they had light, they had heat, they had food and drink and reading matter, they had communication with the outside world; and still Dortmunder was gloomy. "I'm a dead man," he repeated, brooding at the piece of pizza in his hand. "And I'm already buried."

"John, John, you're *safe* here."

"Forever?"

"Until we think of something." Kelp used a fingertip to push pepperoni into his mouth, chewed a while, swigged some beer, and said, "One of us is bound to come up with something. You *know* we are. We're both clutch-hitters, John. When the going gets tough, the tough get going."

"Where?"

"We'll think of something."

"What?"

"How do I know? We'll know what it is when we think of it. I tell you what'll happen: We won't be able to stand it down here any more, and one of us will think of the solution. Necessity is the mother of invention."

"Yeah? Anybody know who the father is?"

"Errol Flynn," Kelp said, and chuckled.

Dortmunder sighed and opened the paper. "If they hadn't slowed the space program," he said, "I could of volunteered for a moon shot. Or the space station. That can't be all scientists and pilots; they're gonna need somebody to sweep up, polish the windows, empty the wastebaskets."

"A custodian," Kelp said.

"A janitor."

"Actually," Kelp said, "custodian is more accurate than janitor. They both come from the Latin, you know."

Dortmunder paused in turning the pages of the paper. He looked at Kelp without speaking.

"I'm a reader," Kelp explained, a bit defensively. "I read a piece about this."

"And now you're gonna tell it to *me*."

"That's right. Why, you in a hurry to go someplace?"

"Okay," Dortmunder said. "Whatever you want." He looked at the editorial page and saw, without recognizing it, the name Mologna.

"Janitor," Kelp told him, "comes from the two-faced Roman god Janus, who was in charge of doorways. So way back in the old days a janitor was a doorkeeper, and over the centuries the job kind of spread. A custodian is from the Latin *custodia*, meaning to take care of something you're in charge of. So custodian is better than janitor, especially in a space station. You don't wanna be doorkeeper in a space station."

"I don't wanna be a squirrel in a tunnel the rest of my life either," Dortmunder said. *Mo-log-na*, he thought, and scanned the editorial.

"Squirrels don't go in tunnels," Kelp objected. "Squirrels hang out in trees."

"That's another piece you read?"

"I just know it. Everybody knows it. In tunnels what you've got is rats, mice, moles, worms—"

"All right," Dortmunder said.

"I'm just explaining."

"That's it, that's all." Dortmunder put down the paper, picked up the phone, and started to dial. Kelp watched him, frowning, until Dortmunder shook his head, said, "Busy," and hung up. Then Kelp said, "What is it? Another pizza?"

"We're getting out of here," Dortmunder told him.

"We are?"

"Yeah. You were right; there was gonna come a time when one of us couldn't stand it any more, and he'd think of something."

"You thought of something?"

"I had to," Dortmunder said, and tried the number again.

"Tell me."

"Wait a minute. May?" Dortmunder whispered again, cupping the mouthpiece, hunching a bit over the phone like a man trying to light a cigarette in a high wind. "It's me again, May."

"You don't have to whisper," Kelp said.

Dortmunder shook his head for Kelp to shut up. Still whispering, he said, "You know the thing? That made all the trouble? Don't say it! Take it with you when you go out tonight."

Kelp looked very dubious. Apparently, in Dortmunder's ear May was also being dubious, because he said, "Don't worry, May, it's gonna be all right. At last, it's gonna be all right."

39

March is just about the end of the winter frolic season in the northeast quadrant of the United States. In the Sleet & Heat Sports Shoppe on lower Madison Avenue, late that afternoon, the staff was busily stashing its leftover stock of toboggans, ski boots, ice skates, parkas, crutches, and flasks to make room for summer fun equipment—sunburn lotion, chlorine, shark repellent, salt tablets, poison ivy spray, bug killer, arch support sneakers, decorator-designed sweatbands, and T-shirts bearing comical messages—when a clerk named Griswold, a chunky, healthy, wind-burned twentyish sports freak, a sailboater and a hang-glider, a mountaineer and a cross-country skier, who was only working here anyway for the employee discount and what he could boost, looked out through his bushy red eyebrows and saw two men slinking into the store: old men, maybe even forty, no wind, no legs, no staying power. Midwinter pallor on their drawn faces. Abandoning the display of Ace bandages he'd been setting up, Griswold approached these two, on his face the smile of superior compassionate pity felt toward all losers by all perfect specimens. "Help you, gentlemen?"

They looked at him as though startled. Then the one with the sharp nose muttered to his friend, "You handle it," and drifted back to stand by the door, hands in his pockets as he gazed out at the overcast late afternoon and the sidewalks full of people rushing to get indoors before the storm.

Griswold gave his full alert attention to the one who would handle it, a slope-shouldered, depressed-looking fellow. Whatever sport he was involved with, Griswold thought, it hadn't done much for him: "Yes, sir?"

The man put his hand up to his mouth and mumbled something behind it, the meanwhile his eyes flicked this way and that, scanning the store.

Griswold leaned closer: "Sir?"

This time the mumble made words, barely audible: "Ski masks."

"Ski masks? Ah, skiing! You and your friend there in-
dulge?"

"Yeah," the man said.

"Well, that's fine. Come right over this way." Leading
the way deeper into the store, past splints and shoulder pads
and groin cups, Griswold said, "You must have seen our ad in
the paper."

"We just happened by," the man said, still talking into
his hand, as though he had a tiny microphone in there.

"Is that so? Then this is your lucky day, if I may say so."

The man looked at him. "Yeah?"

"We're in the middle of our end-of-season ski sale."
Griswold beamed happily at his customer. "Fantastic savings,
right on down the line."

"Oh, yeah?"

The other customer was still back by the door, looking
out, and thus was out of earshot, so Griswold concentrated on
the bird in hand. "That's right, sir," he said. "Now, here, for
instance, are these magnificent Head skis. Now, you know
how much these little beauties would normally set you back."

"Ski masks," the man muttered, not even looking at the
beautiful skis.

"All set for skis?" Griswold reluctantly let the beauties
lean again against the wall. "How about boots? Poles? You
see hanging on the wall there, sir—"

"Masks."

"Oh, of course, sir, that's right here in this display case.
Take your time. We also have more in the back I could bring
out if you—"

"Those two," the man said, pointing.

"These? Of course, sir. May I ask, what color is your
primary ski outfit?"

The man frowned at him: "You gonna sell me these
masks?"

"Certainly, sir, certainly." Whipping out his sales book,
remaining ineffably cheerful and polite, Griswold said, "Cash
or charge, sir?"

"Cash."

"Yes, sir. Let me just get a box for these—"

"Paper bag."

"Are you certain, sir?"

"Yes."

"Very well." Writing out the sales slip, Griswold said, "I take it, this time of year, you're heading up Canada way. Ah, the Laurentians, they're wonderful. Best skiing in North America."

"Yeah," the man said.

"Can't beat the Alps, though."

"Naw," the man said.

"You get a lot of glare that far north. Could I interest you and your friend in goggles? Guaranteed Polaroid—"

"Just the masks," the man said, and handed Griswold two twenty-dollar bills.

"That's fine, then," Griswold said, went away, came back with the change and a paper bag, and as he turned over the customer's purchases made one last pitch: "Cold up there, sir. Now, our guaranteed Finnish Army parkas will keep your vital signs intact down to fifty-seven degrees below, or return with—"

"No," the ex-customer said. Stuffing the bag full of masks inside his coat, he turned away, shoulders hunched, and joined his partner at the front door. They exchanged a glance, then left. Griswold, watching through the glass, saw them pause in the doorway and look both ways before turning their coat collars up, tucking their chins down in, shoving their hands deep in their pockets and skulking away, keeping close to the building front. Odd ducks, Griswold thought. Not your ordinary outdoor-enthusiast types.

Half an hour later, stepping back to admire a just-completed pyramid of tennis ball cans surmounted by an elasticized elbow band, Griswold suddenly frowned, pondered, turned his head, and gazed inquiringly toward the front door. But of course they were gone by then.

40

It was raining. Eleven p.m. Dortmunder emerged from the side-street manhole into a gusty, chilly rain, slid the round cover back into place, and took refuge in the nearest storefront doorway. There were no pedestrians. A lone car squished by. Wind currents eddied in the storefront, flicking tiny cold raindrops in his face.

It was nearly five minutes before a Lincoln Continental with MD plates pulled to a stop at the curb out there. Dortmunder crossed the sidewalk, entered the dry warmth of the car, and Kelp said, "Sorry I took so long. Tough to find a car on a night like this."

"You could of found a car," Dortmunder told him, as Kelp eased the Lincoln forward to the nearest traffic light. "You just had to hold out for an MD."

"I trust doctors," Kelp said. "They're ease-loving people, they know all about pain and discomfort. When they buy a car, they want the best and they can afford the best. You say what you want, I'll stick with doctors."

"All right," Dortmunder said. Now that the chill was leaving his bones, now that he was beginning to dry, he was less annoyed.

The traffic light turned green. Kelp said, "Where is this movie?"

"Down in the Village."

"Okay." Kelp turned right, drove downtown to Greenwich Village, turned left on 8th Street, and parked just shy of the theater, whose marquee advertised "American Premiere— A Sound of Distant Drums." That was the movie May had told Dortmunder she intended to see tonight, telling him about it last night, making small talk while Dortmunder's hand had soaked in the Palmolive Liquid. A call to the theater from their ghost telephone earlier this evening had told them the last show would break at eleven-forty.

And so it did. Beginning at eleven-forty and a half, a trickle of culturally enriched patrons emerged from the theater, grimacing at the rain, making complaining noises at one another, hurrying away through the wind-blown squall.

May was among the last to come out. She stood for a moment under the marquee, hesitating, looking this way and that. Kelp said, "What's she up to?"

"She knows what she's doing," Dortmunder said. "She'll just walk around a while, so we see has she a tail."

"Of course she has a tail," Kelp said. "Probably half a dozen. Some pal of Tiny's. The cops. The Terrorists' Cooperative."

"You're very cheery," Dortmunder said.

Outside there, two nondescript men also stood under the marquee, apparently indecisive as to what to do now that the world of the cinema had been replaced by the world of rain. But then May finally moved on, heading down the block away from Kelp and Dortmunder, and after a minute both dawdling men strolled off in that direction as well, having nothing to do with one another, or with May, or with anything.

"Two," Kelp said.

"I see them."

"If they only knew."

"Don't talk."

"What she's carrying, I mean."

"I know what you meant."

Kelp waited till May and her two new friends were all out of sight in the spritzing darkness, then started the Lincoln and oozed away from the curb. In midblock they passed the two men, who were having some difficulty remaining unaware of one another, and a bit farther on they passed May, walking along like a person with nothing to think about but movies.

Astonishingly, the light at the corner was green. Kelp zipped around to the right, pulled in at the curb, left the engine running but turned out the lights. Dortmunder twisted around, looking back through the water-smeared side windows at the corner, his hand reaching back for the rear door handle.

May appeared, walking purposefully but not hurriedly.

She turned right, continued to walk, and the instant the corner building cut her off from the view of the following men she made a brisk dash for the car. Dortmunder shoved open the rear door, May hopped in, and Kelp accelerated, turning the next corner before switching on the headlights.

"What a night!" May said, when Kelp eased enough on the throttle so she could peel herself off the seatback. "I knew this was you when I saw the MD plates."

Kelp tossed Dortmunder a quick triumphant grin: "See? It's my trademark." Looking in the rearview mirror he said, "Nobody behind us."

May was studying Dortmunder like a mother hen. "How are you, John?"

"Fine."

"You look all right," she said doubtfully.

"I haven't been gone that long, May."

"Have you been eating?"

"Sure I been eating."

"We had a pizza before," Kelp said. He turned another corner—on a red light, illegal in New York City—and lined out uptown.

"You need more than pizza," May said.

Dortmunder didn't want to talk about his dietary habits: "You brought the stuff?"

"Sure." She handed over a small brown paper bag, the kind you carry a sandwich in.

Taking the bag, Dortmunder said, "Both things?"

"You don't have to do that, John."

"I know I don't. I want to. Is it in here?"

"Yes," she said. "They're both there."

Kelp said, "How was the movie?"

"Good. It was about the evils of European influence in Africa in the last part of the nineteenth century. Very interesting soft-focus camera work. Lyrical."

"Maybe I'll go see it," Kelp said.

Dortmunder kneaded the brown paper bag in his hands. "There's something else in here."

"Socks," she said. "I figured, a night like this, you'll need dry socks."

Kelp said, "I don't dare drop you off at your place, May. But within a block, okay?"

"Sure," she said. "That's just perfect." Touching Dortmunder's shoulder, she said, "You'll be all right?"

"I'll be fine," he said. "Now that I finally know what I'm doing."

"Make sure nobody recognizes you," she said. "It's dangerous for you two to be out and around."

"We've got ski masks," Kelp said. "Show her."

Dortmunder took the two ski masks out of his coat pocket and held them up. "Very nice," May said, nodding at them.

"I want the one with the elks," Kelp said.

May unlocked the apartment door and walked into a living room full of cops. "For heaven's sake," she said. "If I'd known there was a party I'd have stopped and bought some cookies."

"Where've you been?" said the biggest, angriest, most rumpled plainclothesman.

"To the movies."

"We know that," said another one. "*After* the movies."

"I came home." She squinted at the clock on top of the TV set. "The movie got out at twenty to twelve, I took a cab, and now it isn't even midnight."

The cops looked a bit uncertain, then pretended they hadn't looked uncertain at all. "If you're in contact with John Archibald Dortmunder—" the big angry rumpled plainclothesman started, but May interrupted:

"He doesn't use his middle name."

"What?"

"Archibald. He never uses the Archibald."

"I don't care," said the cop. "You see what I mean? I don't give a fart."

Another of the cops said, "Harry, take it easy."

"It's getting me down, that's all," the big angry rumpled cop said. "Blitzes, stakeouts, crashing around, everybody on double shift. All over one goddam stumblebum with sticky fingers."

"Everybody," May told him solemnly, "is innocent until proved guilty."

"The hell they are." The cop moved his shoulders around, then said to the other cops, "All right, let's go." Glaring at May, he said, "If you're in contact with John *Archibald* Dortmunder, you tell him he'll be a lot better off if he gives himself up."

"Why should I tell him a thing like that?"

"Just remember what I said," the cop told her. "You could be in trouble, too, you know."

"John would be much *worse* off if he gave himself up."

"That's all right, that's all right." And the cops all pounded their feet on out of there, leaving the door open behind them.

May closed it. "Poo," she said, and went away to open an Airwick.

The jewelry store door said *snnnarrrkk*. Dortmunder pressed his shoulder against it: "Come *on*," he muttered.

snik, responded the door, yawning open. This time, knowing this particular door's wiles and stratagems, Dortmunder already had one hand gripping the frame, so he didn't lose his balance but merely stepped across the threshold into the store, where he stopped to look back at Kelp, standing lookout at the curb in the rain, gazing assiduously up and down empty Rockaway Boulevard. Dortmunder gestured, and Kelp happily squelched across the sidewalk and joined him in the warm interior of the store. "Nice little place," he said, as Dortmunder shut the door.

"This ski mask itches," Dortmunder said, peeling the thing off.

Kelp kept his on; his eager eyes sparkled amid gamboling elks on a field of black. "It sure keeps the rain off," he said.

"It isn't raining in here. The safe's over this way."

The "Closed For Vacation To Serve You Better" sign was still in the front window, and the mustiness of the air inside the store suggested no one had been in it since the cops had arrived Wednesday night to find the Byzantine Fire missing. The store owner was in jail now, his relatives had things other than his shop to think about, and the law had no more use for the place.

Or at least that's what they thought.

"Forty-eight hours," Dortmunder said. "See those clocks?"

"They all say twenty to one."

"That's what they said Wednesday night, when I came in. What a forty-eight hours!"

"Maybe they're stopped," Kelp said, and went over to listen to one.

"They're not stopped," Dortmunder said, irritated. "It's just one of those coincidences."

"They're working," Kelp agreed. He came back and watched Dortmunder seat himself cross-legged, tailor-fashion, on the floor in front of the familiar safe, spreading his tools out around himself. "How long, you figure?"

"Fifteen minutes, last time. Shorter now. Go watch."

Kelp went over to the door to watch the still-empty street, and twelve minutes later the safe said *plok-chunk* as its door swung open. Dortmunder shined his pencil flash in at the trays and compartments, now stripped of everything except the junk he'd rejected last time, and saw one tray full of junky pins—gold-plated animals with polished stone eyes. That would do.

Reaching into his pocket, Dortmunder took out the Byzantine Fire, then spent a long moment just looking at it. The intensity of the thing, the clarity, the purity of the color. The depth—you could look down for miles into that damn stone. "My greatest triumph," Dortmunder whispered.

Over at the door, Kelp said, "What?"

"Nothing." Dortmunder put the Byzantine Fire on the tray with the junky animals; dubious peacocks and lions stared pop-eyed at this aristocrat in their midst. Dortmunder sort of piled the animals around the ruby ring, obscuring it slightly, then slid the tray back into place.

"How you doing?"

"Almost done." *Chock-whirrr*; he shut and locked the safe and spun the dial. His tools went back into their special pockets inside his jacket, and then he got to his feet.

"Ready to go?"

"Just one second." From another pocket he took May's watch and pressed the button on the side: 6:10:42:11. Crossing to the display case, he beamed his pocket flash at the watches behind the glass until he found another of the identical kind, in a small felt-lined box with the lid up. Going behind the counter, opening the sliding door in the back of the display case, he took out this new watch and saw that in the box with it was a much-folded paper headlined INSTRUCTIONS FOR USE. Right. 6:10:42:11 went back on the counter display where he'd originally found it, and the new one with its box and its instructions went into his jacket pocket. And the itchy ski mask went back on his face. "Now I'm ready," Dortmunder said.

43

Every edition of the paper. From the bulldog edition that had come out last night before Mologna had left the city for Bay Shore and home, right up to the late final that hadn't hit the street until he was already back in his office this morning, every last rotten edition of that rotten paper had carried the same rotten editorial. "The Cost Of Blowing Your Top" it was headed, and the subject matter was Mologna's now-famous incident of hanging up on the guy with the Byzantine Fire.

Was it those FBI assholes who'd given the story to the paper? Probably, though it had to be admitted Mologna had one or two enemies right here within the sheltering arms of the NYPD. All morning his friends on the force had been calling to commiserate, to tell him the same thing could have happened to them—and they were right, the bastards, it could have—and to assure him all the pressure in the world had been put on the editors of that rag to drop the editorial from the later editions, but in vain. The bastards had known they were safe, Chief Inspector Francis Xavier Mologna was down, they could kick him with impunity now. "There's nothin lower than a newspaperman," Mologna said, and swept the late final edition from his desk onto the floor.

Where Leon skipped over it on his way in, saying, "Another phone call."

"Friend or foe?"

"Hard to say," Leon told him. "It's that man again, with the Byzantine Fire."

Mologna stared. "Leon," he said, "are you havin fun at my expense?"

"Oh, Chief Inspector!" Leon's eyes fluttered.

Mologna shook his head. "I'm not in the mood today, Leon. Go away."

"He insists on talking with you," Leon said. "I quote—" he made his voice a kind of deep falsetto "—'for our mutual advantage.' That's what he said."

Wait a minute. Was it possible to recoup after all, to make a comeback, to shove that editorial down those craven editors' throats? Mutual advantage, huh? Reaching for the phone, Mologna said, "Which line?"

"Two."

"Record it and trace it and track it," Mologna ordered. His own voice deepening, he said, "I'll *keep* him on the line." Then, as Leon skipped from the room, Mologna said into line two, "Who's this?"

"You know," said the voice.

It was the same voice. "John Archibald Dortmunder," Mologna said.

"I'm not Dortmunder," Dortmunder said.

"Is that right," Mologna said comfortably, settling into his seat for a good long chat.

"The frame won't hold," the voice said. "You'll find out Dortmunder isn't the guy, and you'll keep looking till you find me."

"Interestin theory."

"I'm in trouble," said the voice.

"That's the understatement of the year."

"But you're in trouble, too."

Mologna stiffened. "Meanin what?"

"I read the paper."

"Every son of a bitch reads the paper," opined Mologna.

"We could maybe help each other," the voice said.

Mologna glowered, from deep within his soul. "What are you suggestin?"

"We both have a problem," said the tired, weary, pessimistic and yet self-confident voice. "Maybe together we got a solution."

Leon tiptoed in, hopped over the newspaper on the floor, and put a note on Mologna's desk, reading, "Phone company says untraceable, no such phone." Mologna glared at that, and said to the voice, "Hold it a second." Pushing the *hold* button, he glared at Leon and said, "What the fuck is this?"

"The phone company's bewildered," Leon told him. "They say the call's coming from somewhere south of 96th Street, but they can't track it down. It's just *there*, in their relays."

"That's too fuckin stupid to be believed," Mologna said.

"They're still working on it," Leon said, not with much display of hope. "They said please keep him on the line as long as you possibly can."

"Are you insultin me, Leon?" Mologna demanded. Without waiting for an answer, he pushed the two-line button, and heard a dial tone. The son of a bitch was gone. "Oh, Jesus," Mologna said.

"He hung up?" Leon asked.

"I lost him *again*." Mologna stared at infinity as the phone on Leon's desk outside began ringing. Leon trotted away, and Mologna leaned forward, elbows on desk, head in hands, thinking the unthinkable: Maybe I should retire, like the fuckin paper said.

Leon was back. "It's him again. This time he's on one."

Mologna moved so fast he almost ate the phone. "Dortmunder!"

"I'm not Dortmunder."

"Where'd you go?" Mologna demanded, while Leon danced back out to contact the phone company once more.

"You put me on hold," the voice said. "Don't put me on hold, all right?"

"It was only a second."

"I've had a lot of trouble with phones," the voice said. (Perhaps another voice in the background made a complaining noise.) "So just don't put me on hold. No gizmos."

"No *gizmos*?" Honest rage and accumulated frustration bubbled up within Mologna. "*You're* one to talk, you've been makin a mental case out of me with your telephones."

"I just—"

"Never mind that, never mind that. I call you at a pay phone, right out on the street in the sunshine, you answer the phone, and *there's nobody there!* Right now, right this minute, you're talkin to me big as life, the phone company can't trace the call! Is that honest? Is that playin the game?"

"I just don't like to be on hold," the voice said, sounding sullen.

Which brought Mologna back down out of his luxurious bad temper. "Don't hang up again," he said, squeezing the receiver hard, as though it were his caller's wrist.

"I won't hang up," the voice agreed. "Just so you don't put me on hold."

"You've got a deal," Mologna told him. "No hold. I'll just sit here and you'll tell me your story."

"My story is," said the voice, "I don't want this ruby thing."

"And?"

"And you do. It'll make you the big man again around Headquarters, never mind what they say in the papers. So what I want, I want to propose a trade."

"You'll give me the ring? For what, immunity?"

The mirthless voice said, "You can't give me immunity, nobody can."

"I hate to say it, pal," Mologna told him, "but you're right." And yet, the strange thing was, he felt within himself a desire to help this poor son of a bitch. Some echo in that world-weary voice reached out to him, called out to their common humanity. Maybe it was just because he was depressed after that stinking editorial, but he knew in his heart he was closer to this fourth-rate burglar, in some cockamamie way, than to anybody else involved in the whole case. He pictured FBI Agent Zachary in an interrogation with this clown, and despite himself, his heart just reached out. "So what do you want?" he said.

"What I want," said the voice, "is another burglar."

"I don't follow."

"You're the cops," the voice explained. "You can make up a name, make up a guy, some guy that doesn't exist. Frank Smith, say. Then you announce you got the burglar and his name is Frank Smith and you got the ring back and it's all over. Then nobody's mad at *me* any more."

"Nice try, Dortmunder," Mologna said.

"I'm not Dortmunder."

"The problem is," Mologna went on, "where is this Frank Smith? If we set up a make-believe guy, we've got nobody to show the press. If we set up a real guy, maybe the frame doesn't stick."

"Maybe Frank Smith commits suicide in the House of Detention," the voice suggested. "Such things have been known to happen."

"Too many people involved," Mologna said. "I'm sorry, but there's no way we could work it." He laid out the parameters of the problem: "It would have to be a real guy, with a record, somebody known to the courts and to the underworld. But at the same time, it would have to be a guy nobody's ever goin to find, he'll never come back with an alibi or a— Holy Jesus!"

In sudden hope, the voice said, "Yeah? Yeah?"

"Craig Fitzgibbons," Mologna said, an almost religious awe trembling in his voice.

"Who the hell is that?"

"A guy who will never come around to call us liars, Dortmunder."

"I'm not Dortmunder."

"Sure, sure. I can do your setup for you, that's all. I sit here astonished at myself. Now, what about the *quo*?"

"The what?"

"The Byzantine Fire," Mologna explained.

"Oh, that. You get it back," the voice said, "as soon as you make the announcement."

"What announcement?"

"Police breakthrough. Proof positive the thief with the Byzantine Fire is this fella Craig Whoever. Arrest expected any minute."

"All right. Then what?"

"I get the ring back to you, my own way. Indirect like."

"When?"

"Today."

"And if you don't?"

"Another police breakthrough. Proof positive it *isn't* Craig Thingummy."

"Okay," Mologna said, nodding. Leon came in and made the world's most expressive shrug of incredulity, representing in himself all of the thousands and thousands of employees of the New York Bell Telephone Company. Mologna nodded, waving him away, not caring any more. "I'm in a good mood today," he told the phone. "You've got yourself a deal, Dortmunder."

"Call me Craig," said Dortmunder.

44

Every half hour Dortmunder phoned May, who was staying home from work so she could listen to an all-news radio station ("You give us twenty-two minutes, we'll give you the world," they threatened). Dortmunder would have preferred to be his own listening post, but down here in the telephone company conduit, far beneath the mighty metropolis, there was no such thing as radio reception. As for TV, forget it.

"There's trouble in Southeast Asia," May told him at ten-thirty.

"Uh-huh," Dortmunder said.

"There's trouble in the Middle East," she said at eleven o'clock.

"That figures," he said.

"There's trouble in the Cuban part of Miami," she announced at eleven-thirty.

"Well, there's trouble everywhere," Dortmunder pointed out. "There's even a little right here."

"They have positively identified the thief who stole the Byzantine Fire," she said at noon. "It was just a bulletin, interrupted the trouble in baseball."

Dortmunder's throat was dry. "Hold it," he said, and swigged some beer. "Now tell me," he said.

"Benjamin Arthur Klopzik."

Dortmunder stared across the conduit at Kelp, as though it was *his* fault. (Kelp stared back, expectant, alert.) Into the phone, Dortmunder said, "*Who?*"

"Benjamin Arthur Klopzik," May repeated. "They said it twice, and I wrote it down."

"Not Craig Anybody?"

"Who?"

"Benjamin—" Then he got it. "Benjy!"

Kelp could stand no more. "Tell me, John," he said, leaning forward. "Tell me, tell me."

"Thanks, May," Dortmunder said. It took him a second

to realize the unfamiliar, uncomfortable feeling in his cheeks was caused by a smile. "I hate to sound really optimistic, May," he said, "but I have this feeling. I just think maybe it might be almost possible that pretty soon I'll be able to come up out of here."

"I'll take the steaks out of the freezer," May said.

Dortmunder hung up and just sat there for a minute, nodding thoughtfully to himself. "That Mologna," he said. "He's pretty smart."

"Wha'd he do? John?" Kelp was bouncing up and down in his eagerness and frustration, slopping beer out of the can onto his knees. "*Tell* me, John!"

"Benjy," Dortmunder said. "The little guy the cops wired."

"What about him?"

"He's the guy Mologna says boosted the ring."

"Benjy Klopzik?" Kelp was astonished. "That little jerk couldn't steal a paper bag in a supermarket."

"Nevertheless," Dortmunder said. "Everybody's after him now, right? Because of being wired."

"They want him almost as bad as they want you," Kelp agreed.

"So the cops announce *he's* the guy lifted the ruby ring. He won't come back and say no, it wasn't me. So that's the end of it."

"But where is he?"

"Who cares?" Dortmunder said. "The Middle East, maybe. The Cuban part of Miami, maybe. Maybe the cops killed him and buried him under Headquarters. Wherever he is, Mologna's pretty damn sure nobody's gonna find him. And that's good enough for me." Reaching for the phone, grinning from ear to ear, Dortmunder said, "That's *plenty* good enough for me."

45

Life is unfair, as Tony Costello well knew. He was on the very brink of losing his job as police-beat reporter on the six o'clock news, and it was all because nobody knew he was Irish. It was bad enough that "Costello," though Irish, sounded Italian; but then his mother had had to go and compound the problem by naming him *Anthony*. Sure there were lots of micks named Anthony, but you go ahead and combine "Anthony" with "Costello" and you might just as well forget the wearin' o' the green altogether.

Plus, Tony Costello's additional misfortune was that he was a black Irishman, with thick black hair all over his head, and a lumpy prominent nose, and a short and chunky body. Oh, he was doomed right enough, that he was.

If only it were possible to bring it out into the open, to *talk* about it, go up to some of these dumb micks—Chief Inspector Francis X. Mologna, for instance, *there* was a tub of dolphin shit for you—and say to these fellas, "God damn it to hell and back, *I'm Irish!*" But he couldn't do that—the prejudice, the old boys' club, the whole Irish Mafia that runs the Police Department and always has would have to be acknowledged that way, which of course was out of the question—and as a result all the best scoops, the inside dope, the advance words-to-the-wise all went to that son of a bitch *Scotsman*, that Jack Mackenzie, because the dumb micks all thought *he* was Irish.

"Looks like spring today!" said a pretty girl in the elevator at noon on Saturday, but Tony Costello didn't give a shit. His days as police-beat reporter were numbered, the numbers were getting smaller, and there was nothing he could do about it. A month, six weeks, two months at the outside, and he'd be shipped bag and baggage to Duluth or some damn place, some network affiliate where the police beat was automobile accidents and Veterans' Day parades. Maybe it looked like spring today, maybe last night's drenching rain had been winter's valedictory, maybe this morning's soft breezes and watery sun heralded the new season of hope, but if there was no hope in Tony Costello's heart—and there was none—what could it matter to him? So he snubbed the pretty girl in the elevator, who spent the rest of the day looking rather bewildered, and he stamped down the corridor past all the other busy-busy network employees into his own cubicle, where he asked Dolores, the secretary he shared (for as long as he was still here) with five other reporters, "Any messages?"

"Sorry, Tony."

"Sure," Costello said. "Sure not. No messages. Who would call Tony Costello?"

"Buck up, Tony," Dolores said. She was slender, but motherly. "It's a beautiful day. Look out the window."

"I may jump out the window," Costello said, and his phone rang.

"Well, well," Dolores said.

"Wrong number," Costello suggested.

But Dolores answered it anyway: "Mister Costello's line." Costello watched her listen, nod, raise her eyebrows; then she said, "If this is some sort of prank, Mister Costello's far too busy—"

"Huh," said Costello.

Dolores was listening again. She seemed interested, then intrigued, then amused: "I think maybe you ought to talk to Mister Costello himself," she said, and pressed the hold button.

"It's Judge Crater," Costello suggested. "He was captured by Martians, he's spent all these years in a flying saucer."

"Close," Dolores said. "It's the man who burgled Skoukakis Credit Jewelers."

"Skoukakis . . ." The name rang a bell, then exploded: "Holy shit, that's where the Byzantine Fire was grabbed!"

"Exactly."

"He says—he says *he's*, uh, uh, Whatsisname?" (Not being on the inside track with the boys at Headquarters, Costello mostly got his police news from the radio and had heard

Mologna's announcement in the car on the way downtown.
Oh, it was an uphill fight for Tony Costello every inch of the
way.)

"Benjamin Arthur Klopzik," Dolores reminded him.
"And what he says is, he robbed the place. To prove his point,
he described the store."

"Accurately?"

"How would I know? I've never been there. Anyway, he
wants to talk to you about the Byzantine Fire."

"Maybe to set up a return." A rare smile lightly touched
Costello's features, making him look a bit less like an Irish
bog (or an Italian swamp). "Through me," he said, in won-
derment. "Is that possible? Through *me!*"

"Talk to the man."

"Yes. Yes, I will." Seating himself at his desk, switching
on the tape that would record the call, he lifted his phone and
said, "Tony Costello here."

The voice was low in volume and with a faint echo, as
though the speaker were in a tunnel or something. "I'm the
guy," it said, "that robbed Skoukakis Credit Jewelers."

"So I understand. Klop, uhh . . ."

"Klopzik," said the voice. "Benjamin Arthur—I mean,
Benjy Klopzik."

"And you have the Byzantine Fire."

"No, I don't."

Costello sighed; hope dashed, yet again. "Okay," he said.
"Nice talking to you."

"Wait a minute," Klopzik said. "I know where it is."

Costello hesitated. This had all the characteristics of a
prank or crank phone call, except for one thing: Klopzik's
voice. It was a gruff voice, with a weariness, a many-battles-
lost quality that reminded Costello of himself. This voice
would not pull pranks, would not do dumb stunts for fun.
Therefore Costello stayed on the line, saying, "Where is it?"

But then Klopzik had to go and say, "It's still in the
jewelry store."

"So long," Costello said.

"God damn it." Klopzik's voice sounded really annoyed.

"What's the matter with you? Where you going? Don't you want the goddam story?"

Which stung Costello: "If there *is* a story," he said, "naturally I want it."

"Then stop saying good-bye. The reason I picked you, I seen you on the TV and I don't think you're in the cops' pocket like that guy Mackenzie. You know the one I mean?"

Costello's heart warmed to this stranger: "I do indeed," he said.

"If I give this to Mackenzie he'll give it very quiet to the cops, and they'll do it very quiet, and I'll still be in a jam."

"I don't follow."

"Everybody's on my tail," Klopzik explained. "They're looking for the guy hit the jewelry store because they think I got the ruby, too. But I don't. So what I want, I want a lot of publicity when you get the ruby, so everybody knows I never had it, so they'll get off my back."

"I am beginning," Costello said, "to believe you, Mr. Klopzik. Tell me more."

"I broke in there that night," Klopzik said. "Must of been just after they put the ruby there. I didn't see them or anything, I'm not a witness. I just went in, I opened the safe, I took what I wanted, I saw this big red stone on a gold-looking ring, I figured it had to be fake. So I left it."

"Wait a minute," Costello said. "Are you telling me the Byzantine Fire has been in that jewelry shop the whole time?" He was peripherally aware of Dolores staring at him, openmouthed.

"Absolutely," said Klopzik, with ringing sincerity. "This whole thing has been very unfair to me. It's strained my relationship with my friends, made me the object of a police dragnet, driven me from my home—"

"Hold on, hold on." Costello gazed at Dolores with wondering eyes, as he said to the man he was now convinced was an honest, truthful burglar, "Can you tell me *exactly* where you saw the Byzantine Fire?"

"Sure. It's in the safe, in a tray on the lower right. You know, the kind of tray you pull out like a drawer. It's there with a lot of little gold pins shaped like animals."

"That's where you saw it."

"And that's where I left it. A great big red stone like that in a little jewelry store in South Ozone Park, you got to figure it for a fake, right?"

"Right," said Costello. "So the police—and the FBI, by God, the police *and* the FBI—they all went to that jewelry store, they all searched the place, and none of them saw the Byzantine Fire, and it was *there all along!*"

"Definitely," said Klopzik. "I never had it on my person. I never so much as touched it."

"Let's see." Costello scratched his head through his thick black hair. "Would you be willing to do an interview? Just a silhouette, you know, no names."

"You don't need me," Klopzik said. "The whole point is, I never had nothing to do with that ruby in the first place. Listen, the store's empty now, it's closed, there isn't even a police guard. What you do, what I think you ought to do, if you don't mind my giving you advice—"

"Not at all, not at all."

"I mean, it's your business."

"Give me advice," Costello instructed.

"Okay. I think you oughta go out there with Skoukakis' wife, or whoever has a key and the safe combination, and bring along a camera, and you can film the stone just lying there on that tray."

"My friend," Costello said warmly, "if I can ever do you a favor—"

"Oh, you're doing me a favor," Klopzik said, and there was a click, and he was gone.

"Lordy lordy lordy," Costello said. He hung up and sat there nodding thoughtfully to himself.

Dolores said, "From the half I heard, he says he never took it."

"It's still there." Costello looked at her, wide-eyed with hope. "I believe him, Dolores. The son of a bitch was telling the truth. And I am going to ram the Byzantine Fire so far up those dirty bastards at Police Headquarters, they'll have red molars. Get me—" He stopped, frowning, gathering his thoughts. "Skoukakis is in jail; he has a wife. Get me the wife. And put an order in for a remote unit. Oh, and one thing more."

Dolores paused, halfway out the door toward her own desk. "Yes?"

"You were right before," Tony Costello told her, with a big happy grin. "It *is* a beautiful day."

46

Dortmunder was still hidden in the telephone tunnel during the six o'clock news, so he watched the repeat that night at eleven. By then the news was generally known, the heat was off, and Dortmunder was free to sit in his own living room on his own sofa and gaze in contentment at his own television set. The cops, the crooks, the terrorists and spies and religious fanatics, all were gone away now, somewhere else, minding their own business. Dortmunder was, at last, out from under.

Since the O.J. had been the subject of a very severe police raid last night, immediately after Benjy Klopzik's spy equipment had started picking up CB, and was therefore now closed for repairs, Dortmunder had agreed that Stan Murch's postponed meeting could take place here in the apartment tonight, with only one proviso: "I need to watch the news at eleven."

"Sure," Stan had said, on the phone. "We'll all watch."

And so they did. Stan Murch, a blocky, ginger-haired man with freckles on the backs of his hands, was the first to arrive, shortly before eleven, saying, "I was out in Queens anyway, so I took Queens Boulevard and the Fifty-ninth Street Bridge and came down Lex."

"Uh-huh," Dortmunder said.

"The trick is," Stan said, "you don't turn off on Twenty-

third like everybody else. You take Lex down to the end, you
go around Gramercy Park over to Park, you save a lot of
lights, a lot of traffic, and you got a *lot* easier left turn onto
Park."

"I'll remember that," Dortmunder said. "You want a
beer?"

"Yes, I do," Stan said. "Hiya, Kelp."

Kelp was on the sofa, watching the end of a prime time
rerun. "Whadaya say, Stan?"

"I bought a car," Stan said.

"You *bought* a car?"

"A Honda with a Porsche engine. The thing flies. You
gotta throw out a parachute to stop it."

"I believe you."

Dortmunder came back with Stan's beer as the doorbell
rang again, and this time it was Ralph Winslow and Jim
O'Hara, the two guys Dortmunder had met at that first
aborted meeting at the O.J. Everybody said hello, and Dortmunder went back to the kitchen for two more beers. On his
return, handing them out, he said, "We're all here but Tiny."

"He won't be along," Ralph Winslow said. He didn't
sound unhappy.

"Why not?"

"He's in the hospital, sick. When the cops raided the O.J.
last night, Tiny was alone in the back room with all those files
listing everybody's crimes and whereabouts and whatnot for
Wednesday night."

Dortmunder stared. "Did the cops get all that?"

"No," Winslow said. "That's just it. Tiny barricaded the
door. He didn't have any matches to burn the papers, so he
ate them. All of them. The last batch, the cops broke through
the door, they're beating on him with sticks, he's chewing and
swallowing and fighting them off with chairs."

O'Hara said, "The word is, he'll be in the hospital at
least a month."

Winslow said, "Some of the guys are getting up a collection. I mean, that was a noble act."

"I'll contribute," Dortmunder said. "In a kind of a way, I
almost feel some responsibility, you know?"

"I hate to tell you this, John," Stan Murch said, "but even I began to think you were the guy with the mark on his back."

"Everybody did," Dortmunder said. His eye was level, his voice was clear, the hand holding his beer can was steady. "I don't blame people, it was just one of those things. It was circumstantial evidence."

"Don't tell *me* about circumstantial evidence," O'Hara said. "I did a nickel-dime once for hitting a lumberyard safe, and all they had on me was sawdust in my cuffs."

"That's terrible," Kelp said. "Where'd they nab you?"

"In the lumberyard office."

"So that's the way it was with me," Dortmunder said. "And the bad mood everybody was in, I didn't dare come out and explain myself."

"Wasn't that Klopzik something?" Winslow grinned in something like admiration, swirling his beer can as though it might contain ice cubes to clink. "Working both sides against the middle. Wired up for the cops, *and* he knocked over that jeweler all along."

"Without even taking the Byzantine Fire," O'Hara said. "A thing as famous as that. How dumb can you get?"

"It's coming on," Kelp said.

So they all sat down to watch. The anchorman introduced the story, and then a tape of the six o'clock report came on, starting with Tony Costello seated at a desk in front of a blue drape, his head and right hand bandaged but his expression cheerfully triumphant. He said, "The intensive nationwide search for the missing Byzantine Fire came to an abrupt and bizarre end this afternoon, back where it all started, at Skoukakis Credit Jewelers on Rockaway Boulevard in South Ozone Park."

Then there was film of the jewelry store, showing Tony Costello—unbandaged—with a woman identified as Irene Skoukakis, wife of the store's owner. While a voice-over narration explained that Benjamin Arthur Klopzik himself, object of the most intense manhunt in New York Police Department history, had phoned this reporter earlier today with the astounding revelation that had led to the recovery of the miss-

ing priceless ruby ring, the camera showed Costello watch
Irene Skoukakis unlock the front door and then go inside and
open the safe. The camera panned in close as she pulled open
the tray—here's where the voice-over repeated Dortmunder's
story about having left the Byzantine Fire behind—and there
it was, the goddam ruby, big as life, huge and gleaming and
red amid the little gold menagerie.

Next there came a cut back to the bandaged Costello at
his desk, saying, "Naturally, we informed both the police and
the FBI the instant we'd verified Klopzik's story. The result
was, to this reporter at least, something of an astonishment."

More film: official cars slamming to a stop in front of the
jeweler's, uniformed and plainclothes cops milling around.
And then the astonishment: film showing a man identified by
the voice-over as FBI Agent Malcolm Zachary, on the sidewalk in front of the store, in the process of punching Tony
Costello in the face. Costello went down and, while the camera ground on, the stout form of Chief Inspector Francis X.
Mologna came running into the scene and started kicking the
fallen journalist.

"Holy cow," Dortmunder said.

Another cut back to Costello at his desk, now looking
serious and judicious and just a teeny bit sly. "This unfortunate incident," he told the viewers at home, "merely shows
how tempers can fray when the heat is really on. This network has already accepted the apologies of both the Federal
Bureau of Investigation and the Mayor of the City of New
York, and I personally have accepted the apologies of Agent
Zachary and Chief Inspector Mologna, both of whom have
been granted leaves of absence for reasons of health. In all of
this, only one minor element truly pains me, and that was
Chief Inspector Mologna's reference to this reporter, in the
heat of the moment, as a 'dirty Wop.' Now, it happens that I
am one hundred percent Irish extraction, though of course
that doesn't matter one way or the other, but even if I weren't
Irish, even if I were Italian which I am not, or if I were a
Scotsman, such as Jack Mackenzie, my opposite number on
another network, no matter what ethnic group I might belong

to, I would still have to be saddened and distressed at this
suggestion of ethnic stereotyping. Even though I'm Irish, I
must say I would be proud to be called a Wop or a Dago or
anything else such misguided people might choose to say.
Some of my best friends are Italian. Back to you, Sal."

"Right on," said Andy Kelp, as Dortmunder switched off
the set.

"Okay," Stan Murch said. "Enough of the past. We
ready to talk about the future?"

Kelp said, "Sure we are. You got a caper, Stan?"

"Something very nice," Stan said. "I'll drive, of course.
Ralph, there's some very tough locks to get through."

"I'm your man," Ralph Winslow said.

"Jim, Andy, there'll be climbing and carrying."

"Sure thing," Kelp said, and Jim O'Hara, his prison
gray already receding, said, "I'm ready to get back into action. Believe me."

"And, John," Stan said, turning to Dortmunder, "we're
gonna need a detailed plan. You feel good?"

"I feel very good," Dortmunder said. It was too bad he
couldn't tell the world about his greatest triumph, but since
his greatest triumph had turned out to be no more than a
circle in which he wound up putting his most magnificent
haul back where he'd found it, maybe it was just as well to
keep it to himself. Still, a triumph is a triumph is a triumph.
"In fact," he said, "I would say I'm at the beginning of a
lucky streak."